Triplets

Becky's Problem Pet

HOLLY WEBB

SCHOLASTIC

Scholastic Children's Books
An imprint of Scholastic Ltd
Euston House, 24 Eversholt Street
London, NW1 1DB, UK
Registered office: Westfield Road, Southam, Warwickshire, CV47 0RA
SCHOLASTIC and associated logos are trademarks and/or registered trademarks of
Scholastic Inc.

First published in the UK by Scholastic Ltd, 2004
This edition published by Scholastic Ltd, 2014

Text copyright © Holly Webb, 2004

The right of Holly Webb to be identified as the author
of this work has been asserted by her.

ISBN 978 1407 14477 1

British Library Cataloguing-in-Publication Data.
A CIP catalogue record for this book is available from the British Library.

Printed and bound by CPI Group (UK) Ltd, Croydon, CR0 4YY
Papers used by Scholastic Children's Books are made from wood grown in
sustainable forests.

1 3 5 7 9 10 8 6 4 2

www.scholastic.co.uk

Chapter One

Becky Ryan curled up in the corner of the blue-painted garden shed, and sighed contentedly. It was Saturday afternoon, she'd *finally* finished her homework and she had the new issue of her favourite magazine to read. She waited for Vanilla, the calmest and most readable-with of her four guinea pigs, to snuggle herself down properly on her lap, and opened up *Practical Pets*. It wasn't the only animal magazine she read – depending on how many cat toys and guinea-pig treats she'd bought that month, she got a whole load of others as well, *Your Cat*, *Animals and You*, whatever looked good. But she always, always bought *Practical Pets*. Becky and her best friend

Fran had once tried to explain to the other two Ryan triplets why it was so much the best. Annabel had said she thought it looked boring – the other animal magazines had loads more cute pictures, and wasn't that what they wanted?

"No," Becky had exclaimed in disgust. "I mean, I've got no problem with the cute pictures—"

Here Annabel and Katie had snorted with laughter, which was fair enough, as Becky's bit of the big cork noticeboard in their bedroom was absolutely covered in fluffy kittens and Golden Retriever pups.

Becky had grinned shamefacedly. "Ha ha. What I mean is, this one has good photos, but it actually tells you useful stuff too. Like which sort of food is best, and how to stop your cat eating too much, that kind of thing."

Annabel had gazed pointedly at Orlando, the Ryans' big ginger cat, who was sprawled on Becky's bed, enjoying the attention he was getting from Fran, and Becky had sighed irritably.

"Yeah, well. It doesn't work if the cat just goes out and nicks the next-door neighbours' dinner, does it, Orlando?" Becky had said sternly.

Becky shuddered as she remembered the whole embarrassing episode, apologetically stroking Vanilla, who wriggled crossly as her comfy seat moved. Orlando had turned up his nose at his bowl of *very* expensive diet cat food, supposed to help him lose weight, and stalked out. Ten minutes later he'd sauntered back in, looking smug – and he'd been closely followed by a furious ringing at the doorbell. It was Mrs Saunders from next door, holding a packet of sausages. A *half-empty* packet of sausages. . .

Becky grinned. It *had* been quite funny really, though she hadn't thought so at the time, and neither had Mum, who'd had to grovel to Mrs Saunders, whose Yorkshire terrier (a bad-tempered, snappy little dog, that even Becky didn't like very much) would never have *dreamed* of behaving in such a terrible way, and on, and on, and on.

She picked up *Practical Pets*, wondering what this month's featured pet was going to be – last month's had been lizards, and she hadn't been very keen. She'd shown the article to Jack, one of the boys at school, though, and he'd been gripped. He had a pet lizard that he kept in his bedroom. Becky supposed it was quite an interesting pet, but she preferred things with fur. She couldn't imagine curling up to read a magazine cuddling a lizard. . .

Ooohhh – the huge long featured-pet article was about rats! Becky really liked the idea of a pet rat – they were so cute, and a bit more cuddly than mice or hamsters or gerbils, because they were bigger. She flicked quickly to the right page. Awww – look at this one's gorgeous whiskers! She just had to have some!

Vanilla eeped crossly. She seemed to think that Becky was not paying her sufficient attention, which Becky wasn't, as she was entirely absorbed in the rat article. She gave Vanilla an absent-minded stroke, and went back to looking at the recommended rat cage. It was more like a rat palace, it was so enormous! Apparently rats were very intelligent, and needed lots of things to play with, and lots of handling if you wanted them to be tame and friendly. Becky sighed. Pocket money was in short supply after splashing out on reflective collars for Orlando and their other cat, little black Pixie. A semi-detached rat bungalow was way out of her price range at the moment, let alone this one that the magazine recommended, with the tunnels and multi-gym. Although it wasn't long until Christmas. Hmmmm. Maybe it was time to start introducing Mum to the joys of rats?

Becky had been campaigning for the Ryans

to get a dog, but she was beginning to think it wasn't going to happen. Mum wasn't showing any signs of changing her mind – she still said that their garden wasn't big enough, and that with three children, two cats and four guinea pigs they simply didn't have the space for a dog, especially not a big dog like the Golden Retriever Becky really wanted. She'd tried getting Fran to bring her retriever, Feathers, round, so as to show Mum how cute and gorgeous and well-behaved he was, but Feathers unfortunately had no sense of timing, and he always did something naughty just when Mrs Ryan was watching. Becky was gradually coming to the conclusion that a dog was as unlikely as the pony she'd spent months dreaming about when she was seven. She wasn't actually giving up, of course, but she might think about transferring her attentions to rats for a bit.

Suddenly a massive thump startled her out of her daydream of unwrapping a deluxe rat-home on Christmas morning, and she bounced upright, nearly squashing Vanilla, who made a noise that was as near to swearing as a guinea pig can, and nipped Becky crossly on the thumb.

"Ow! Sorry, Vanilla baby, I know it wasn't your fault." Becky stroked the sulking guinea pig soothingly, and glared at the door of the shed, which was now opening to reveal her sisters. "What did you do – oh, stupid question." Becky spotted the football under Katie's arm, and Annabel doubled up with giggles. "For somebody who's supposed to be brilliant at football, you 'accidentally' hit this shed an awful lot. Vanilla bit me, you know!"

"Sorry!" replied Katie cheerfully, and Annabel added, "It'll make up for the millions of times that Orlando and Pixie have bitten me and Katie when they never, ever bite you. Come on, we want to go and mail Dad."

Katie nodded. "I've got loads to tell him

about our match last night, and we haven't sent him a joint email for ages."

The triplets' parents were divorced, and their dad was currently working on an engineering project in Egypt. He came back every so often to see them, but not often enough, and Katie especially missed him, because he was really into sport like she was and understood how she felt about it. They had last seen him at half–term, and now he wouldn't be back until after Christmas, so they were doing a lot of emailing – they talked on Skype too, but it was tricky to catch him when he was out on site so much, and with the time difference as well. Dad had bought them a digital camera back in the summer, too, so they also kept him up to date with loads of photographs.

Becky heaved herself up off the shed floor and opened the hutch that Vanilla shared with Maisy. She skilfully slipped the wriggling guinea pig inside, and shut the door carefully – Maisy and Vanilla had been known to make escape bids before now.

Then the triplets headed off through the garden to the house, and raced up the stairs to the converted loft where the computer lived. Katie got the proper chair, simply because she'd run fastest, and the other two dragged up a huge beanbag that Mum had invested in recently for this very purpose – *three* computer chairs was an extravagance, she'd said.

"Ooof!" said Becky, as Annabel flumped down half on top of her. "What is this? Let's cripple Becky day? Watch it, Bel!"

"Shut up, you two," said Katie bossily, turning on the computer. "Start thinking about what you want to say to Dad."

"No point," Annabel shrugged. "It'll be ages before you've finished telling him boring football stuff, won't it? Besides, I'm best just – letting it all out. It's more creative that way." She smiled with all the smugness of someone whose English teacher had told her she had a brilliant imagination. Annabel had chosen to take it entirely as a compliment, but Katie and Becky were pretty sure that Mr Marshall had meant it just a little bit sarcastically as well. She *had* just told him a very long and involved story about why it was absolutely necessary for her to talk to Saima during their English comprehension session.

Katie shook her head disgustedly and started to type a detailed account of her first practice with the County Under Thirteens squad, which she'd just been picked to join.

It's brilliant, Dad! Mrs Ross is a really good coach, but it's just her, and the county squad have got loads of coaches and assistants and people, so it's like there's somebody watching your every move (scary!) and telling you how to make it even better. I'm one of the youngest (though there is one girl who's only ten, she's like some kind of genius) so I won't get to play in a proper match for a while (specially with my leg still not being right yet), but the training is going to be brilliant, and you never know, I might get to be a sub.

She went on to describe the exact exercises and warm-ups she'd been shown to strengthen her leg – she'd been injured in a girls versus boys match at school a few weeks earlier. She knew that Dad would be interested – Mum and Becky and Annabel did their best, but even Mum's eyes glazed over sometimes, and Bel had recently put a two-minute limit on any football conversation. Katie's section of the email was pretty long, and she only stopped because Annabel's fake snoring was getting too annoying to bear.

"Shut up, Bel! OK, it's your turn. Honestly, you're so impatient."

"Well, this was meant to be an email from

all of us, not just you writing a book." Annabel flounced up from the beanbag and seated herself on the chair with exaggerated care – just because she knew it would annoy Katie. She smoothed out her pink denim skirt, and shook her long hair over her shoulders so it wouldn't get in her way. She'd curled it on bendy rollers the night before and it was being a bit mad today. In a very cool way, of course – somehow Annabel didn't have bad hair days.

It was another ten minutes before Becky got anywhere near the computer, but she didn't mind. Mailing Dad every week was a very them thing to do, and even if they were telling him about all the stuff that made them so different to each other, somehow it was important that they did it together. She stayed curled on the beanbag, deep in her magazine, while Katie did stretches and Annabel typed frantically.

Eventually, Katie gave herself a little shake

all over, and decided she was done with exercising. She wandered up to Annabel and peered over her shoulder at the screen.

"Oh, Bel! Not *again*!"

"What?" demanded Annabel indignantly.

"Josh Matthews from Year Eight — you're obsessed!"

Annabel had been typing a description of Josh for Dad. He was her and Saima's latest pick for most gorgeous boy in school, and Katie was sick to death of the sound of his name.

"Don't worry, Katie," Becky called from the beanbag. "She'll have forgotten him by next week. It'll be Kieran, or Tom or Matt. You know."

"Kieran!" screeched Annabel in disgust. "I don't *think* so! Did you not see what he was wearing when we saw them in town last week? Urrrgh. Anyway, Josh is really nice, and clever, and he just happens to be incredibly good-looking as well. But that's not what's important."

Katie snorted in disbelief. "Whatever. Hurry up, it's Becky's turn."

Becky extracted herself from the depths of the beanbag, and went over to the computer to read Annabel's contribution.

"Katie's right, Bel. You and Saima *are* obsessed. I don't even think he's that nice-looking."

"And what would you know about it?" Annabel sounded sulky. She didn't like having her judgement questioned. In the short time the triplets had been at Manor Hill, she'd shown herself to be the fashion guru of their year (although one of the other girls in their class, Amy Mannering, who completely couldn't stand the triplets, wouldn't have agreed) and she tended to predict who all the Year Seven girls would be mooning over that week – it was whoever *she'd* been admiring the week before. "If it doesn't have fur and a tail you aren't interested, so you're not exactly worth listening to on the subject!"

She rattled off a last sentence with a bad-tempered flourish, and got up. "There you go – tell Dad about the last nice dog you met in the park."

Becky flushed and looked hurt, and Katie folded her arms, glaring at her sister. "Bel! That's really mean – just because Becky and me aren't as mad about boys as you and Saima, you don't have to be so horrible."

Annabel flushed as pink as Becky and scowled. "Well, Becky was horrible first."

"Oh, stop it!" Becky broke in. "It doesn't matter – no, Katie, leave it!" She could see that Katie was about to lay into Annabel again. "Anyway," she grinned, "I'm not going to email Dad about dogs, I've got loads of stuff about rats to tell him." As she'd expected, that completely distracted Katie and Annabel.

"Rats?"

"Urrgh!"

"They're not urrgh, they're gorgeous, look!"

And Becky stood up and thrust the magazine under Annabel's nose. "Look how cute this black and white one is!"

Annabel shuddered. "Becky, it's a rat! It's, it's . . . vermin. They're all dirty, and smelly!"

Becky grinned and shook her head. "Oh, you're hopeless!" She sat down at the computer. "What do you think, Katie?"

Katie looked over Becky's shoulder at the magazine that she'd put down next to the keyboard.

"Ummm. I suppose it's OK. I don't much like that long pink tail, though, Sort of – wormy. But its fur's quite pretty."

"Good, 'cause what I'm telling Dad now is that I'd like rats for Christmas, so you two are just going to have to get used to the idea!" Becky turned back to the keyboard decisively and went on typing:

There's a big article in *Practical Pets* this month about rats. They're really clever,

16

and friendly, if you look after them properly and handle them lots. Did you know that the pet kind are called fancy rats, and there are loads of different colours and types you can get? Even a Siamese one, like cats! I'd like a blue rat. The one in the magazine is a really gorgeous dark greyish–blue with lovely black eyes. Annabel says they're all horrible – she's looking at the magazine right now and making sick noises.

Becky rolled her eyes at her sister as she typed this, and tried to ignore Annabel's disgusted comments. She finished off her section of the email and clicked on send, then grabbed back her magazine.

Katie grinned at her. "You'll have to be careful, you know – Pixie and Orlando and the guinea pigs are going to get really jealous if all you talk about is rats. They'll think you don't love them any more!"

Becky made a "don't be so stupid" face, but clattered down the stairs at high speed to find Orlando and Pixie and make a big fuss over them. . .

Chapter Two

Becky spent the rest of the weekend daydreaming about pet rats, and doing more research about them on the internet. Everything she read made her more and more keen to have her own.

Mum didn't seem to think the idea of rats for Christmas was too silly, although she did go a bit pale when Becky showed her the price of a really good rat cage (on some pages she'd printed off from a fancy rats website). And she made a similar comment to Katie's – that she wasn't sure Becky would have enough time to look after all the animals. Becky was convinced it would be OK, though, even if she did have to get up an hour earlier to fit in all the playtime the rats needed. Mum seemed pretty impressed when she said that.

Becky was keen to get to school on Monday morning and tell Fran about her rat plan – so keen that she managed to leave *Practical Pets* sitting on the kitchen table next to her toast plate, rather than sticking it in her rucksack as she'd meant to. But it didn't stop her reciting the article practically word-perfect to Fran as they sat hunched up by the chestnut tree in the playground. Being November it was fairly cold, and the triplets and their friends were muffled up in scarves and gloves, and huddling together.

"I'll bring it in tomorrow – I can't believe I left it at home. You need to see the pictures, they're so lovely. Rats look really cuddly. Do you remember when we went to that big pet shop in town a while ago and they had some?"

Fran sighed. "Oh yes. I'd love to have one."

"I thought that too, but apparently you

shouldn't ever have just one — they're too friendly for that, so you've got to have at least two or they get lonely — isn't that sweet?"

This time Fran's sigh was even louder. "Doesn't matter anyway. I'm not going to get any more pets ever, I don't think."

Becky looked surprised. "Why? I thought your dad liked animals. Wouldn't he like rats?"

"It's not rats, it's *anything*. He reckons he's got enough on his plate with Feathers."

Becky grinned. She knew Feathers, and Fran's woebegone face could mean only one thing. "OK. What did he do? Did he chew through another electric wire?" she asked, with interest. Feathers was a gorgeous dog, and Becky was hugely envious of Fran having him, but she could see that he didn't exactly make life easy.

"Dad's trying to train him not to jump up at the table," Fran explained. "We've tried gently pushing him down, and spraying him with a

JF/233 4479

plant-mister, and all the normal kinds of things, and nothing was working, so Dad emailed a "pet problems" website for advice. They said there was an absolutely foolproof way to stop him – Dad was over the moon. So we tried it yesterday. Dad made this huge sandwich" – Fran took her hands out of her sleeves (she'd forgotten her gloves) and indicated a really massive sandwich – "two big slabs of bread, a really thick layer of that strong horseradish sauce he likes, and some mustard, and he'd even gone to the supermarket and got some extra hot chilli sauce, and he put that in too." Fran sighed. "According to the guy on this website, the dog jumps up, sees this yummy-looking sandwich, gulps it down, and gets a massive shock 'cause it tastes horrible. So afterwards it thinks that anything it gets off the table might taste the same, and it stops doing it."

"Well, it *sounds* like it should work," said Becky doubtfully. "But I suppose it didn't?"

"Nope. Feathers waltzes into the kitchen, sniffs out the sandwich, and Dad and I carefully pretend we're not looking. He jumps up and grabs it, then settles down on the floor to gobble it up. From what the website said, practically from the first bite he should have been dashing for his water bowl like his mouth was on fire, but Feathers ate – the – whole – thing! And then he licked his lips, looked round, and jumped back up again to see if he'd missed anything. Chilli sandwiches are obviously his favourite thing."

Becky giggled. "Oh dear. Well, at least you know what to get Feathers for Christmas now."

"Yeah, chilli-flavoured dog chews, if they exist. But you see what I mean? I don't think now is the right time to be asking Dad for any more pets. He was muttering about dog shelters again last night."

Becky looked shocked. "He wouldn't!"

Fran shrugged. "No, I don't think so. Most

23

of the time he really loves Feathers. We're just not very good at training him. And it's funny, 'cause Golden Retrievers are meant to be really easy to train. Sometimes I think Feathers is just a really strange-looking dachshund, or something."

Fran looked at Becky, and they both creased up at the idea of Feathers actually being a sausage dog in disguise.

"What?" asked Annabel curiously, looking at them heaving with laughter. "What are we missing?"

"You – you – wouldn't think – it was all that funny," gasped Becky. "Dog joke. Honest."

Annabel rolled her eyes, and she and her friend Saima went back to watching the Year Eight boys playing football – with Josh Matthews captaining one side, and looking very good indeed.

Katie was watching too, but not for the same reason. Josh and quite a few of the other Year Eight boys were in the boys' junior team that her team had beaten so brilliantly earlier on in the term, and she and Megan, who played in goal, were having a very critical look at their ball-skills.

"Sloppy," commented Megan with her head on one side, and her arms folded, in an unconscious imitation of their coach, Mrs Ross.

"Mmmm," agreed Katie, tutting as another of the boys completely lost control of the ball.

"As if you could do any better," said a sneery voice, and Katie and Megan wheeled round.

Max Cooper, of course. The boy who'd deliberately fouled Katie in that boys v girls match, and made her miss the final of the schools league because of the torn muscle in her leg.

Katie gave him a poisonous little smile. "Yeah, Max, we could. We proved it, and we don't have to cheat like you. Get lost."

Max looked stumped for a moment, but

recovered quickly. "Yeah, and what if I don't? You going to get your *mum* on to me? Poor little Katie needs Mummy to look after her," he sneered.

After Max had deliberately injured Katie, the triplets' mum had phoned up his dad and had a real go at him.

Max's dad had been very apologetic and grounded Max for ages. In fact, Mrs Ryan had got off the phone with his dad and said she felt sorry for him and Max more than anything else – Max's mum had died two years ago, and Mr Cooper was bringing him up on his own. Unfortunately, even though the triplets knew they ought to be sympathetic, it didn't make Max any easier to like – especially now he could call Katie a "Mummy's girl" in every other sentence.

Seeing that Katie was about to explode and that might get them all into trouble, Megan joined in. "Why don't you go and ask if you can play? You certainly need the practice.

Oh, I forgot, there's no point is there? 'Cause Mr Anderson's banned you from playing in the team for, oooh, how long was it again?"

Max stomped off, bright scarlet by now, and the girls giggled.

"You know," said Annabel, "I just don't understand why he bothers trying to pick fights with you, Katie. You always make him look a prat, so why does he come back and do it again?"

"Bad memory." Megan nodded wisely. "I bet in half an hour he'll have forgotten what we said entirely, and he'll think he was really clever. It's a boy thing."

Just then the bell went, so they hauled themselves and their bags across the playground to their deliciously warm classroom, and started thawing out while they waited for Miss Fraser to come and do the register.

Becky and Fran were trying to draw a picture of Feathers the sausage dog on a bit of scrap paper – Fran was brilliantly good at drawing, and Becky was offering advice.

"Bigger ears, definitely."

"You think? Mmm, probably."

"That's really good," said a shy voice from over their shoulders.

Becky and Fran both peered up. It was David Morley, a boy the triplets were friendly with – he'd only moved into their area that year, and Becky had felt sorry for him not knowing anybody, so she'd invited him to their birthday party during half-term. He was very sporty, and good at football without being an idiot about it like Max was, so Katie liked him too. Annabel just thought his hair needed sorting out. . .

Becky and David got on really well, but they were both naturally shy. Becky sometimes worried whether David actually *liked* talking to her, or whether he was just being polite.

"Oh, hi David. It's cute, isn't it? She's so

good at drawing." Becky nudged Fran. "She'll never admit it, though. It's meant to be a kind of mixture between Fran's dog and a dachshund. You remember Feathers – you met us walking down the high street with him?"

Fran blushed. "He's not likely to forget, Becky. It was so lucky you had some money on you, David. I thought that woman was going to drag me and Feathers to the police station."

David grinned at her. "It was her own fault for leaving her shopping on the pavement next to a huge dog while she was nattering to her friend. Anyone with more than two brain cells could have seen he'd have that packet of biscuits out of there in no time."

"We should train him and Orlando to work together," Becky put in. "We could make a fortune."

Miss Fraser chose that moment to walk in and tell everybody to sit down, and David gave

Becky and Fran a quick grin, and disappeared over to the other side of the room. Becky looked down very carefully at Fran's picture, and wondered why she was feeling disappointed because they hadn't had a chance to chat for very long.

Saima had asked her a couple of weeks before whether she fancied David, as she seemed to spend so much time chatting with him. It had been a bit of a shock – Becky hadn't really thought about David like that before. But once Saima had mentioned it, she'd found it difficult to get it out of her mind, even though she'd told Saima she wasn't interested at all.

She kept an eye out for David through the rest of the day, as she wouldn't have minded chatting to him some more, but he seemed to be avoiding her.

That afternoon Katie was staying for football practice with Megan, and Megan's mum was going to run her home afterwards (Mrs Ryan didn't mind the triplets walking to and from school in a group, but she wasn't keen on them being on their own). So Annabel and Becky walked home with Saima and Fran, dawdling along and chatting.

When they got to the high street and were just coming up to the pet shop, Becky suddenly interrupted Annabel and Saima's long discussion about exactly which Hollywood actor Josh Matthews looked most like.

"Can we pop in here, really quickly? Pleeease? I just want to ask Mr Davies if he ever has any rats."

"Becky! Why have you suddenly turned into a rat-freak?" asked Annabel mock-crossly. "Oh, OK, I don't mind – if you two haven't got to get home dead on time?"

Saima shook her head, and Fran said, "No, and I love going in here."

"We're not staying more than five minutes, though, got it?" cautioned Annabel. But she

31

was already talking to Becky and Fran's backs as they disappeared into the shop.

Mr Davies's shop was a lot better than some pet shops. It wasn't very big, but anything he didn't have he could order for you, and he was very knowledgeable. Becky came in regularly to buy stuff for the cats and guinea pigs, and Fran's dad had asked him about Feathers lots of times, so Fran was soon telling him the chilli sandwich story while Becky nosed around the cages.

All the cages were spotlessly clean, and the animals looked well cared for. Becky skimmed past hamsters, gerbils and mice while waiting for Fran to finish telling her story, so she could ask about rats. Then she got to the last cage on the bottom row, and squeaked with delight.

"Mr Davies! You've got some rats! Oh, look Bel, white ones!"

Annabel wandered over and peered gingerly into the cage, and made a face.

"Becky, they do not look any better in real life. Rats are *horrible*." She nudged Saima. "Aren't they?"

Becky gave Saima a pleading look, but she shook her head.

"Sorry Becky, I don't like them either. Especially those – they've got nasty red eyes. They look spooky."

"Pink-eyed whites," said Mr Davies, smiling at Annabel and Saima's evident disgust. "You two aren't fans, then?"

Fran looked over his shoulder. "That's really weird. Becky was coming in to ask if you ever sold rats, and you've got some. Aww, look at them playing!"

The rats were tussling with a cardboard toilet roll tube, and as they watched, one of them shot right through the middle, giving the others a shock. Even Annabel and Saima giggled.

Mr Davies grinned at Becky. "Do I sense a customer?"

"Maybe – but not until Christmas. I

should think these will have gone by then, won't they?"

"Probably, but if they're popular, then I'll get some more. You never know."

Becky sighed. "They're so cute. I really would love some. We'd better go, though. Mum'll be wondering where we are. See you soon, Mr Davies."

For the rest of the way home, anyone listening would have been very confused. It was gorgeous Josh Matthews on one side of the conversation, and gorgeous rats on the other. . .

Chapter Three

Becky remembered to bring *Practical Pets* to school the next day, but Fran had a dentist's appointment in the morning, so it wasn't until their history lesson that she and Becky were sitting together, and able to look at the magazine. Miss Fraser was a bit late, so they spread out the magazine on the table between them and proceeded to coo over the photos. *Finally*, Becky thought − it was nice to have someone to appreciate them properly!

Miss Fraser had split the class into project groups at the beginning of term. Becky and Fran were with two boys called Jack and Robin that Fran knew from her old school.

Jack leaned across the table and peered at

the magazine. "Is that the same one you lent me? That had the lizards in? Are there any lizards this time?"

Becky smiled at him. "No, this month it's rats. Hopefully I'm going to get some for Christmas."

"Are you? I've got some rats, did you know?"

Becky gazed at Jack, completely gobsmacked. "Really? Rats? I thought you just had a lizard."

Jack shook his head. "Nope. I've got two rats as well. I got them a few weeks ago, off a mate of mine's brother, and I'm going to breed them."

"Wow." Becky was impressed, though a little surprised. From all the research she'd done over the weekend, she knew that breeding rats was pretty difficult – you needed to know lots about genetics, and which rats to mate with which, if you were going to do it properly. She hadn't really thought of Jack as the kind of person who'd want to do all of that. "Have you got space for them?"

"Yeah, in my bedroom. I'm turning it into a rat-farm. There'll be hundreds of them soon."

"But how are you going to afford all the cages and everything? And the food?"

"Oh, I'll manage," said Jack vaguely. "It won't be a problem once I start to sell them."

Becky started to ask Jack why he suddenly wanted to breed rats, but gave up and just looked at him worriedly. It didn't sound to her as though Jack had a clue what he was doing. But maybe he did and he just wasn't very good at explaining about it? She really, really didn't want to be rude – she wasn't like Katie, who'd happily say what she thought, quite often without stopping to wonder if it was the best thing. And it wasn't as if it was actually any of her business! She smiled at Jack, and tried to sound as though she was just interested in a friendly sort of way. "So what are your rats like? What colours are they?"

"Umm, one's a sort of browny colour and one's white with black bits. Like that one." Jack pointed to a picture of a hooded rat in Becky's magazine, and Becky and Fran leaned over to admire it – it was white, but with a black head and shoulders, so it looked like it was wearing a black furry hood.

Unfortunately, neither of them had noticed that Miss Fraser had come in, and that she was now standing right next to them. Jack had noticed her out of the corner of his eye, but he didn't have time to warn the girls, and Robin had just been gormlessly staring into space – he explained later that he'd been trying to work out how to get to the next level of his current PlayStation game.

"Becky? Fran?"

As soon as they heard Miss Fraser's icy voice, Becky and Fran twisted round guiltily to look up at her.

"Would I be correct in thinking that that is not your history textbook?"

"Umm, yes Miss Fraser," muttered Becky apologetically.

"You know, of course, that if I'm delayed reaching your lesson, you're supposed to read ahead in your textbook?"

Becky and Fran decided not to point out that absolutely *no one* in the classroom had been reading ahead in their textbook – everyone had been chatting. The thing was they'd all had the sense to have the textbooks out, so they could at least *look* as though they were reading when Miss Fraser arrived. Becky and Fran had been too interested in the magazine to remember simple safety precautions. . .

"I will take this –" Miss Fraser picked up the magazine between finger and thumb as though it were something disgusting – "and I *might* let you have it back at your next lesson."

She glared at them both, and swept back to her desk.

Becky stared very hard at the tabletop in front of her, and tried not to cry. She hated being told off – even though she could see that Miss Fraser had been quite nice really. If it had been Mr Hatton, their French teacher, they would probably have been in detention, writing an essay on rats in French or something. She was focusing so hard on the table that she didn't see Katie and Annabel's sympathetic and encouraging glances from their groups over the other side of the room. Unfortunately, though, she could still hear, and Amy Mannering and her two cronies, Cara and Emily, were at the perfect distance for nasty, hissing comments that Miss Fraser wouldn't hear but Becky certainly would.

"Ahhhh, poor little Becky!"

"Look, she's going to cry!"

"No big sisters to look after her, so she gets in trouble." Amy sniggered. "It must be awful to be that useless, don't you think?"

Becky felt Fran glaring furiously over her shoulder at her tormentors, which made her feel slightly better, but obviously Fran didn't want to risk answering back – Miss Fraser still had her eye on them.

She was surprised to catch another quiet voice, from the same direction. "Shut up, Amy. She's not useless, and everyone else in the class likes Becky – they think you're a stuck-up little princess, so just leave her alone."

That got Becky out of her table-obsessed trance in a second. She whisked her head round quickly, and saw David giving Amy a look that reminded her of Katie – something along the lines of "Yeah, so now what are you going to do about it?" Amy looked gobsmacked. She and Cara and Emily just ignored David in history. Miss Fraser might have put him in their project group, but that didn't mean they had to speak to him, and he never spoke to them unless he had to. Amy had always assumed this was because he was too in awe of her to dare, but she was now realizing that maybe that wasn't the case. . .

David spotted Becky watching, and flashed her a quick, embarrassed grin, which she returned before turning back and concentrating very hard on her textbook. Neither of them noticed Amy staring at them thoughtfully, or the sly, calculating expression that quickly passed over her face. So things were like that, were they? Well, David Whatever-his-name-was had better watch out – nobody spoke to her like that.

Annabel and Katie made a beeline for Becky at the end of the lesson.

"Are you OK?" Katie asked her, in a resigned kind of voice – Becky could be so sensitive.

"Oh, yes." Becky nodded.

Her sisters looked at her, surprised – they'd been expecting Becky to be upset after being told off in front of everybody. If they'd known about Amy's nasty comments they would have been even more confused. But Becky seemed amazingly calm – except that they didn't know she was bubbling inside. It had been so nice of David to stick up for her like that! She was used to Katie and Annabel defending her, but they had to, they were her sisters – and they were quite likely to tell her off for being a wimp after they'd done it. She hadn't got the impression that David thought she was silly – he'd just seemed to think that Amy was mean. She felt like giggling at the memory of Amy's shocked face.

They all wandered over in a group to the dining hall for lunch – the triplets with Fran, Saima and Megan. Normally they aimed for one of the tables by the windows, which gave them a good view of the whole room, but Annabel and Saima shepherded everybody to one of the middle tables for some reason.

Katie was confused. "Bel, why do we want to sit here? Look, we're really close to Mr Hatton" – their very strict French teacher was on lunch duty – "can't we go where we always go?"

43

"Sssshh!"

Becky giggled, and nudged Katie. "Look who I can see!"

"Oh." Katie sounded completely disgusted. "What a surprise. Now we even have to eat lunch next to Josh Matthews?"

"Will you be quiet? He'll hear us – just sit down and *shut up*, Katie!"

Annabel was starting to sound fraught, and Saima's normally perfect face was set in a scowl, so Katie sighed, and did as she was told.

They got out their lunches, and waited for Fran to come back from the hot lunch queue with something fairly horrible-looking. The school dinners weren't actually that bad, but they certainly didn't look great, and it was fun to tease Fran about them, as she didn't really mind.

Fran arrived back with her tray – and everyone peered at it with interest.

"Cheese?" asked Annabel, innocently. "A

new kind they've been growing in the kitchens for a while?"

"Ha–ha. Get glasses, Bel. Anybody else want to admit they don't know what fishfingers look like?" Fran said mildly.

There was a general chorus of "Oh, so *that's* what it is!" and Fran shook her head and grinned.

Annabel and Saima went back to the magazine that they were using to camouflage the fact they were really watching Josh. They kept giggling attractively every so often.

"What are you reading, Bel?" Becky peered over at the article. "Is it one of those *My Most Embarrassing Moment* things?"

"Ooh, yes, they're really funny, read it out," said Megan, taking a big bite of her sandwich.

Annabel went a bit pink – she'd had a lot of teasing from Becky and especially Katie about Josh already. But Saima wasn't worried.

"It isn't that sort of article. It's about making yourself look attractive. Boys like girls with a good sense of humour, so you have to laugh when you're around a boy you like."

Katie looked incredulous. "You mean the pair of you are fake-laughing to make Josh Matthews think you're funny?"

Saima nodded. "Mm-hm."

"That is *so* sad. I'm sorry, Saima, but it is."

"I don't see why you have to pretend to be funny, anyway," put in Becky. "You *are* funny, both of you. Why don't you just act how you do normally? We're always getting told off for making too much noise in here 'cause you said something really funny and we're all laughing, Bel."

Annabel and Saima exchanged glances, and sighed.

"It's not the same thing," Annabel explained, in a voice that suggested she was about ten years older and wiser than Katie and Becky.

"It's about – well, it's about attracting the *right* kind of attention. Just trust me."

The triplets' table were so focused on Annabel and Saima that they failed to spot they had a visitor. Max was forced to cough to attract their attention, which was annoying.

Katie turned round to look at him. "Oh, what do *you* want?" she said, sounding bored and slightly irritated, which just ruffled up Max even more.

Megan grinned. "Told you yesterday it wouldn't take him long to get over it."

Max ignored this – as Megan had thought, he was quite good at blocking out what he didn't want to hear. He smiled sweetly at Katie. "I haven't come to talk to you – I want to talk to your sister."

"What do you want to talk to me for?" asked Annabel in disgust. "I certainly don't have anything to say to *you*," she added sniffily.

"Not you either, Little Miss Perfect."

Max's voice was becoming positively sugary – he knew he was about to get the kind of reaction he wanted. When he finally looked at Becky and saw that she was doing a very good impression of a petrified rabbit about to be eaten by a boa constrictor, all bug-eyed and shaky, he couldn't hide his satisfaction.

"Wh-what?" Becky stammered. However often her sisters and her mates laughed about Max being stupid, and however much she agreed with them, she still found him scary. She couldn't just laugh off his insults like Katie and Annabel, and she found it very difficult to keep calm enough to think of anything smart to say back to him. At least she wasn't on her own – she could feel her sisters and Fran and the others bristling, like angry cats.

Max smiled. "I just wondered – I've been talking to Jack, you see, and he told me about his rats. I noticed in history that you were talking to him about them as well, and I just wondered–" He paused.

"What?" snapped Katie. "Get on with it!"

Max ignored her completely, and focused a charming smile on Becky. "I just wondered if you knew what he was breeding them *for*?"

Becky gazed at him, the rabbit still hypnotized by the snake, and said waveringly, "Um, to sell? Isn't he going to sell them to a pet shop, or – or put ads in a magazine, or something?"

Max's smile intensified into a grin. "Oh no. It's very difficult to make money doing that. No, Jack's got a much simpler idea. I think it's really clever." He beamed at her.

"Wh–what's he going to do?" whispered Becky, transfixed by Max's mean smile.

Max crouched down and put his elbows on the edge of the table, then rested his chin on his hands. Katie and Annabel would normally have told him to stop contaminating their food, or something like that, but by now they just wanted to hear what he was going to say. Max lowered his voice confidentially, and everyone leaned in to hear him – he was in his element. "He *is* going to sell them to a pet shop, but not the way you think. He's going to sell them to the place he got his lizard, in Stallford – the exotic animals shop."

"What would they want rats for?" asked Annabel, disbelievingly. "Rats aren't exotic. Don't be stupid."

But Becky knew exactly what Max meant, and her eyes filled with tears. "Oh no! He wouldn't!"

"What?" asked everybody else, confused – Becky might be super-sensitive, but they totally couldn't see what Max had said to upset her.

"Oh yes," said Max silkily. "It's a brilliant way to make money, *I* think. Those places pay loads for decent snake food. Nice and fresh. Juicy. Still running about."

"Don't!" wailed Becky. "That's so horrible!"

"And sometimes the snakes, and the big lizards and things, they want something a bit bigger than a mouse, but not like a *full-grown* rat, so baby rats are just perfect. . . Anyway," – Max smiled round at all the girls – "I thought you might like to know, that's all. Sorry if I've put you off your sandwiches, Becky." Then he wandered back to his own table, casting satisfied glances over his shoulder at the scene he'd left behind.

Chapter Four

The triplets' table were left in stunned silence for a moment, but it was soon broken by Katie, who took one look at Becky's face and immediately tried to undo some of the damage Max had caused.

"Honestly, Becky, don't listen to him – it's probably not even true," she said hopefully.

But Becky was really upset, and she wanted to find Jack right away. The others persuaded her not to – at least not until after she'd calmed down.

"We're right, Becky," Annabel assured her. "You don't want to talk to *anyone* looking like that. You look half mad."

From their worried faces, the rest of the

table seemed to agree, so Becky decided she'd better wait for a bit.

But by next morning she'd made up her mind. Of course, she knew that really she was being silly – the exotic pet shop people were going to get their walking snake food from somewhere, whatever she did, but she just couldn't bear the thought that Jack's baby rats were going to be the ones.

So at registration on Wednesday, she left the others watching her anxiously and forced herself to go across to where Jack and Robin were sitting with some of the other boys, discussing PlayStation games. Even though she knew Jack quite well, it was a bit daunting.

Fran caught her up while she dithered. "I thought I'd come with you. What are you going to say to him?"

Becky looked embarrassed. "I haven't really got that far." She wasn't very practised at arguing – Katie would just storm in and tell Jack that he wouldn't dare to do something so horrible, but Becky didn't think that simple bossiness was really something she could carry off. She was hoping just to – well, she wasn't quite sure *what* she was hoping, but she knew that if she didn't get on and do it now, she'd slink back to her seat and never pluck up the courage again.

"Hi Jack."

Jack turned round from telling Robin that there was no way he could ever beat his time on that race track, because he was useless at the bends, and gave Becky a "What?" look. Actually he was a bit embarrassed, and just trying not to show it – the triplets still had a kind of celebrity status at Manor Hill, and even though Becky (he was *fairly* sure this was Becky, because Fran was with her) was less intimidating than Katie or Annabel, he still didn't want to look an idiot in front of all his mates. Unfortunately, Becky had absolutely no idea that she was scaring him, she was far too nervous herself even to consider the possibility.

"Um, hi," said Becky again. Then she looked helplessly at him, and then round at Fran, while she tried to work out what to say next. Jack just stared at her, and Fran wasn't much help either. Finally Becky pulled herself together.

"Max told us about your rats. That you're not going to breed them as pets, I mean. You're – you're not really going to sell them for snake food are you?" she finished hopefully. Maybe Max had just been trying to upset her after all?

"Course I am," said Jack stubbornly. "It's a brilliant idea. Snakes are really popular pets. Loads of people need rats for them – probably more than want rats as pets. Who'd want a pet *rat*?"

"I would!" squeaked Becky in a hurt voice. "They're lovely. Please Jack, think about it – those lovely little furry rats. You'll feel awful, sending them off to be eaten!"

Fran nodded vigorously. "You couldn't do it!"

"Typical girls!" Jack grinned round at his friends, who smirked back. "You're so babyish. This is a business proposition, Becky, it's not for fun. And I don't feel bad about the rats – why should I? I feed Godzilla crickets all the time" – Godzilla was Jack's pet lizard – "why should I have a problem with snakes eating rats? Because they're *furry*. It's just like a girl to think that makes a difference," he added sneeringly.

Becky was getting cross now, and that helped her arguing. "Actually, baby rats aren't furry at all, they're bald and ugly and they have weird blue lumps where their eyes are going to be. They look horrible, but I'd still love them, and I think you're being totally heartless!"

"Well, they'll be furry by the time they get eaten," Jack snapped back.

Becky gave him a Look – then sighed. She could see there was no point in this. "You really think it's going to work – that you'll make money out of them?" she asked sadly.

"Definitely. I've got it all worked out." Jack's pride in his brilliant business plan suddenly won out over his irritation at being lectured. He wanted to show off. "Look, come and see if you like, both of you. After school this afternoon – I'll show you the rats, and their cage and everything. I'm not being cruel to them, Becky – I look after them. The babies will have a really good life until they go to the pet shop."

Becky shuddered. Somehow that almost made it worse – she could just imagine all those happy little rats, with no idea what they were really living for . . . *urrgh*! But she still very much wanted to see Jack's pair. And maybe seeing them would give her some idea of how to stop Jack's terrible plan?'

"Ummm, all right. I'll borrow Bel's phone and check if it's OK with my mum." Becky didn't have a mobile, but Annabel had begged and pleaded to be allowed one, and their mum had finally given in – provided Annabel paid for it. Annabel was fairly generous about lending it, although she did tend to demand favours in return.

Becky and Fran trailed back to their table, feeling down. Fran looked apologetic. "Sorry Becky, I wasn't much help. I just couldn't think what to say except 'Don't do it!' and I don't think that would have been much use."

"Don't worry, it's not your fault, I couldn't think of much to say either. And I don't think anything would have worked except for a guaranteed reason why rats won't make Jack any money, do you?"

Manor Hill didn't let students have phones turned on except at break and lunch (or that was the theory), so Becky asked Bel if she could borrow her mobile at breaktime.

"Why?" asked Annabel, vaguely. She'd been deep in an excited conversation with Saima about the end of term show — a list had just gone up for auditions, and they were both planning to try out.

"Jack says me and Fran can go round and see his rats after school — I just want to know if it's OK with Mum."

Katie looked worried. "You're going to go and see them? But Becky, won't that just make you more upset?"

Annabel and the others looked as though they agreed with her, and Becky shrugged.

"Maybe. But I'd still like to see them. Wouldn't you, Fran?"

"Mmmm — then at least we'll know he's not feeding them on chocolate, or something stupid. I wouldn't put it past him."

Katie and Annabel exchanged glances. "Well, if Jack doesn't think his mum will mind, I think we should come too," Katie said firmly.

Even though she was feeling depressed, Becky smiled to herself. Katie was doing her protective big sister act again. Well, it wouldn't do any harm — and the more exposure Annabel got to cute rats, the better, as far as Becky could see. She shrugged again. "OK. Anyway, we should check with Mum at break."

Mum was fine with the plan – in fact, her work was obviously going well, because she suggested that any of the triplets' friends who wanted to could come back to their house for a bit afterwards, if their parents didn't mind picking them up. Annabel and Saima, who had some credit on her phone for once, did fairly well at break with Fran and Megan bribing them with chocolate biscuits for phone time.

Jack said his mum was fine with them all coming, though Becky suspected that she didn't actually know she was getting Jack, Robin, the triplets *and* three others.

This suspicion was confirmed by the expression on Jack's mum's face when she opened the door to eight people that afternoon. Jack's little sister was delighted and desperate to come and play with all these exciting new big children, but Jack was firm. "No, Susie! Mum, you've got to keep her downstairs. We're going to let the rats out and you know what Susie's like."

He led the stampede upstairs, hard-heartedly ignoring Susie's wails. When they got to his room he explained, "She's a complete nightmare. I've had to put these special safety locks on Godzilla's vivarium and the rat cage, otherwise she'd be in here playing with them as soon as Mum's back's turned, and I'd never see any of them again, probably. She wants to dress them up and put them in her dolls' house. Honestly."

The others nodded wisely, and Saima put in, "My sister's hamster got out once, and my dad had to take the floorboards up. He was furious."

By this time they were all gathered round the big table under the window where Godzilla's big heated tank stood next to a rather less plush-looking rat cage. It wasn't huge, and Becky was looking at it worriedly. She didn't want to start in on Jack straight away, but she just didn't think it was going to be big enough for a mother and possibly twenty babies! (She'd been amazed when she'd read that it could be as many as that.) And what was Jack going to do with his male rat when the babies came? She didn't think it was a good idea to keep him in the same cage – she'd have to check on the net.

Then the big mound of shredded tissue in the corner of the cage, which had just been twitching occasionally up until now, suddenly erupted. A whiskery face poked out, sniffing, and looking around with interest.

"That's One, he's the male," said Jack over his shoulder – he was undoing the locks on Godzilla's tank and getting the lizard out, murmuring to him admiringly. Godzilla was a leopard gecko, and Becky could see that he *was* very handsome, with his spotted head and dramatic colouring, but she just wasn't that interested in lizards.

"One?" asked Fran, confused.

"Yes, I'm not giving them proper names –

like I keep telling you girls," Jack explained loftily, "this is a business. One and Two are not pets. They're money-spinners."

One was mostly white, but his head and shoulders were very dark brown, and Becky could easily tell that he was a hooded rat. He was gorgeous, and had the most intelligent-looking eyes. He was quickly followed by Two, who was a lovely rich red-brown, and had enormously long wobbly whiskers.

Fran looked at Becky. "Wow! I've never seen a rat that colour, isn't she sweet?"

Becky was in love. "Is she a cinnamon, Jack? She's so pretty! Can we hold them?"

Annabel and Saima, who'd been peering into the rat cage in a sort of horrified fascination (and trying not to get too close to Godzilla either), took a very quick step back. They had no desire to be anywhere near those things without a good solid cage in between. In fact, preferably one that was a lot more solid than Jack's.

Becky giggled, then turned back to Jack. "Please?" she asked hopefully, and Fran looked eager.

"Sure, if you're careful." Jack was enjoying showing the rats off – even if he didn't like them that much, and he had absolutely no idea whether Two was a cinnamon or a curry powder – they were his, and he liked people admiring them.

He handed Godzilla to Robin, then opened the rats' cage and carefully cupped his hands round One, lifted him out and passed him to Becky, who cradled him gently. Then he passed Two to Fran.

"Be careful with her – she's probably going to have her babies any day now."

Becky looked worriedly at Two – was it OK to pick her up if she was pregnant? Oh, well, it was too late now, and Two certainly didn't seem to mind.

"Babies? Really?" Fran gazed at Two who was sniffing her hands with interest, and showing signs of wanting to climb up her arm and investigate the rest of her. One was already sitting on Becky's shoulder, and seemed to be very interested in her bunches.

"Yeah, I've had them in the same cage since half-term when I got them, and rats are only pregnant for twenty days, so I don't reckon it'll be long." He smirked, anticipating his little goldmine growing.

Becky and Fran looked at Two again. She *was* beautiful, and she was also very slim. She didn't look pregnant at all! They exchanged a thoughtful glance, and Becky retrieved One from where he was obviously considering abseiling down her back via her hair. She held him in one hand and tickled his tummy gently, which he seemed to love, and she and Fran exchanged another thoughtful look.

Katie looked at her watch. "Sorry, you two. I think we ought to get back — we told Mum we wouldn't be long. Thanks for showing them to us, Jack."

Becky looked disappointed. "None of the rest of you want a hold? They're ever so tame. Jack must be playing with them loads." She watched Jack carefully as she said this, and, as she'd expected, a slightly worried look passed over his face. She had a horrible feeling that he wasn't handling One and Two much at all.

Katie and Megan got as far as stroking the rats, but didn't want to hold them – Megan explained that it wasn't because she didn't like them, she was just worried because they were so lively and wriggly. What if she dropped one, or held it too tight?

Becky and Fran put One and Two back in the cage, and Jack did up the locks. Annabel and Saima eagerly led the way down the stairs, and said super-polite, relieved goodbyes to Jack's mum, and Susie, who looked as though she was intending to make Jack's life a misery for the rest of the week.

Strangely, Becky and Fran seemed quite happy to leave as well – Katie had been expecting an argument when she'd suggested it was time to go. And why did Becky look as though she was trying not to laugh? Katie hurried them down the garden path at high speed – it was time to find out just what was going on!

Chapter Five

Becky and Fran just wouldn't stop giggling, and it was driving the others mad.

"What is it with you two?" Katie asked, standing with her hands on her hips in the middle of the pavement, and glaring at them in exasperation. "What's so funny?"

"Was there something wrong with those rats?" Megan wondered, intrigued.

"No," said Becky, then looked at Fran and cracked up all over again. This time she laughed so much she could hardly breathe, and she started making strange choking noises, and went bright scarlet.

Annabel was mortified. "Becky, stop it! People are *looking*!" Normally she liked to be the centre of attention, but not because her identical triplet was doing an impression of a crazed beetroot. Unfortunately her pleas had no effect whatsoever on Becky, although she had at least stopped making the wheezing noises.

"Let's get home," said Katie, shaking her head. "She needs a glass of water."

"Yes, and if she doesn't shut up," said Annabel, death-staring Becky, "I'll be pouring it over her head! Get a grip, will you?" She gripped her sister's arm and started to march her in the direction of home, while the others trailed behind, infected by Becky and Fran's giggles, even though they had no idea why they were laughing.

By the time they got into their road Becky seemed to have recovered, apart from subdued giggles every time she looked at Fran. But they were still refusing to say why they were being so mad.

"When we get home," sniggered Becky. "We'll show you, I promise."

The triplets rushed their friends through polite hellos to Mrs Ryan, and stuffed biscuits and drinks into their hands, then they all galloped upstairs to their room, and Annabel and Katie installed Becky on her bed and ordered her to talk – now.

Becky looked round, patted the bed beside her to invite Fran to sit too, and then groped around on the floor beside the bed for some stuff she'd printed off from the net.

"Becky!" wailed Annabel. "Stop messing about and *tell* us!"

"I am!" Becky protested. "No, seriously, I need these to make you understand. It would be easier with my *Practical Pets* magazine, but Miss Fraser's still got that, so this'll have to do."

"There! Look!" squeaked Fran, pointing at one of the pages.

"Oooh, yes." Becky checked that everyone was looking suitably desperate, and smiled. "OK. You know that Jack's big plan is to breed baby rats, right?"

"Yes, of course we do! That's only what you've been having hysterics about since yesterday lunch!" snapped Annabel.

Everybody in the room gave her surprised looks, and she went pink. "Sorry! I just really want to know what's going on!" Annabel was fairly terrible at keeping secrets herself, and she absolutely hated it when she felt that someone wasn't telling her something.

"Well basically, Fran and I were laughing because there's no way that Jack's plan is ever going to work. There aren't going to *be* any babies."

Katie looked confused. "Why not? He's got two rats."

Becky grinned. "He certainly has."

Katie wasn't looking any less confused by this answer, until suddenly her face cleared, and a delighted sparkle came into her eyes. "Oh, you don't mean. . ."

"*Oh* yes," chorused Becky and Fran, beaming.

"What?" yelped Annabel. "Somebody *tell* me!"

"Look." Becky waved her sheets of paper at Annabel, Saima and Megan, and they peered over. "You see these diagrams? That's how you tell if you've got a male rat or a female rat. They had the same sort of thing in the magazine, only with photos so it was a lot easier to tell. Jack was going on about how Two was going to have the babies soon, but she didn't look pregnant. She was really skinny for a rat actually, I don't think he's feeding them right—"

"Becky!"

"OK, OK! So when Fran and I got to hold Jack's rats I looked at them both to check. . . Two's a girl all right – but so is One."

"He's got two *girl* rats?" Megan said slowly.

"Uh-huh. So I'd say the chances of him breeding any snake snacks are pretty low."

The giggles that had been affecting Becky and Fran ever since they left Jack's house now spread to everybody, and it was a good while before they all recovered.

Finally Becky took a deep, calming breath, and reached under her bed for a packet of jellybeans she'd been saving for a special occasion. This was definitely it. She handed them round, and soon everyone was too occupied with chewing for more than a few quiet sniggers.

"Wow." Annabel shook her head. "How could he be that stupid?"

Becky grinned at her. "Like you would have known!"

"Yeah, but I'm not trying to make millions out of rat-breeding – thank goodness. That's such a boy thing to do, it really is."

Katie raised her eyebrows. "Excuse me, what's Josh Matthews?"

Annabel looked patient, as though Katie was being deeply stupid. Then she exchanged an annoying little smile with Saima – a sort of "never mind she'll grow out of it one day" look, a look that it was a good thing Katie missed due to searching for the last orange jellybean.

"Josh Matthews is a *very* gorgeous boy, Katie – and just because I like him it doesn't mean I don't know that most boys are complete idiots."

Katie just shrugged, as though she thought Annabel was crazy, and she simply couldn't be bothered to think through her mad logic – which was pretty much the case. She turned back to Becky. "How come Jack thinks he's got a boy and a girl? Didn't someone tell him when he got them?"

Becky shook her head. "He got them off a friend's brother. Maybe he didn't know either – or maybe he was just having a laugh, telling Jack they were a pair. He probably thought it was really funny."

The jellybean-eating session was interrupted by Mrs Ryan shouting up the stairs. "Megan! Your mum's here!"

"Oh, why does she always have to be on time for everything?" moaned Megan, heaving herself off Katie's bed. "See you tomorrow, everybody."

Saima's dad arrived just as Megan and her mum were heading down the garden path, so when the triplets went back upstairs after saying goodbye it was just them and Fran – the triplets were going to walk her back, as she lived really close.

Becky lay down on her bed facing the others, and put her chin in her hands. "I've just thought of something," she said worriedly. "I'd only been able to think about how funny this all was before, but what's going to happen now?"

"What do you mean?" Fran asked, a confused look on her face. "Nothing's going to happen! That's why it's so funny!"

Katie made a face. "Oh, yeah, I see what you're getting at, Becky. How long is Jack going to wait for his baby rats to turn up?"

"And what's he going to do if they *don't*?" Becky stuck her thumbnail in her mouth and nibbled it worriedly!

"Becky, don't do that," snapped Annabel, and Becky guiltily whipped her hand from her mouth – Annabel could sound very like their mum at times – and then looked crossly at her sister.

"It's my nail, why can't I chew it? I'm worried!"

"Oh fine, just don't blame me next time you want to paint your nails and they look disgusting."

Becky gave Annabel a "you're so weird" look, stuck her thumbnail back in her mouth and spoke round it.

"I don't know how long Jack's going to wait – I mean, he's doing this because he thinks it's going to be easy money."

Fran had sobered up. "You're right. And I don't think he's looking after them properly either. They're too thin, and that cage wasn't very clean. It's not fair – they were so friendly and gorgeous!"

Annabel made a kind of snorting noise, and then withered slightly under a combined glare from Fran and Becky.

"What we're trying to say is, they're really lovely tame rats now, but if he doesn't handle them and play with them every day they'll stop being so friendly," Fran explained.

"Mmm, it won't take long for them to go all wild again. The next time he wants to show them off to someone, they might bite him. If that happens, he'll probably just go into a sulk, give up on the whole thing and give One and Two straight to the exotic pet shop." Becky kicked her feet into the bed frustratedly.

Katie tried to cheer them up. "He might not. I mean, he looks after his lizard really well, doesn't he?"

"Yes but he loves that lizard, and he couldn't really care less about the rats – that's the problem, he's got no time for looking after *them,* he'd rather play with Godzilla." Becky sighed miserably. It was so unfair! Some boy's cruel joke on Jack – and now the rats were paying for it.

Fran looked at her watch. "I'm sorry, I need to get back soon – Dad'll have a go at me about my homework if I don't. Is that OK?"

"Course." Becky rolled off the bed, and Katie and Annabel got up too.

They wandered down the stairs and grabbed their coats. "We're taking Fran home, Mum," called Becky.

"Back in ten minutes," added Katie.

"OK, well, tea'll be ready soon, so make sure it is ten minutes," came the answer from the kitchen.

All the way to Fran's house, she and Becky worried about One and Two, until Katie and Annabel were sick to death of hearing how gorgeous they were, and how much Jack didn't deserve them.

And on the walk back, Becky was totally silent – she had a horrible feeling she was going to have to confront Jack again. . .

Chapter Six

Becky went to school on Thursday knowing that she couldn't simply march up to Jack and tell him that he wasn't looking after his rats properly. For a start, he wouldn't care! That was the whole problem. She needed a plan – when she went to talk to him the day before, she'd worked up her courage just enough to get her across the classroom, but she hadn't actually thought about what she was going to say when she *got* there. Today, she needed to say something that might actually make him listen. She just had no idea what that was.

The triplets and their friends were chatting while they waited for Miss Fraser to come and take the register. Becky was stroking her cheek with the end of one of her bunches, and thoughtfully looking sideways at Jack and his friends, while listening with half an ear to the conversation going on around her. Saima and Annabel still had the magazine that they'd been looking at on Tuesday, and they'd gone back to the article on how to make boys like you.

"'Be nice to them'?" Katie sounded disbelieving. "Well, that's an amazing idea – if you're nice to boys they might like you – wow!"

"It's not just being nice," said Annabel patiently. "It's flattery. It's different. Being interested in stuff they're interested in, getting them to talk about it. Not that it's going to be much use," she added moodily. "Apparently Josh asked out that girl Julianne in Year Eight with the dark red hair." She caught Katie's smirk and added crossly, "And we know you think it's all stupid so you needn't bother saying so."

Saima was reading the article again. "This bit in the bubble says not to forget it can be a good way to make boys do what you want, as well," she said thoughtfully. "Like flattering them to make them think something's their idea, I suppose."

Becky was still staring sideways, but about thirty seconds after Saima's comment, she processed what she'd actually said and turned back, her eyes wide open and hopeful. "Oooh, Saima, please can I have a look?"

Everyone looked at her, amazed, and eventually Annabel came out with what they were all thinking:

"*Why?*"

Becky blushed. "Well, not in a boyfriend kind of way, but I was just thinking it might help me get Jack to look after his rats better. I don't know, maybe I could convince him he wants to, somehow?"

"We might have known," sighed Annabel. "It was too much to hope that you might be interested in my magazine for anything normal like making a *boy* like you. No, of course, you want help with a rat."

Becky smiled sweetly at her. "Two rats, actually. Just give me the magazine, Bel." And she tweaked it out from under Annabel and Saima's noses, and stared at the article very carefully with her chin in her hands, to hide that she was still rather pink. . .

Fran looked over her shoulder. "Do you think you can actually convince Jack that he wants to look after them properly?" She sounded rather disbelieving.

Becky shrugged. "It's the best idea I've had so far. I'm not quite sure how to do it, but it's got to be better than yelling at him, don't you think?"

"Oh, I don't know. . ." Katie grinned.

"I don't do yelling as well as you," retorted Becky. "You got the bossy bit of me, we all know that — it isn't fair."

Fran was looking thoughtful. "Actually, it might not be such a bad idea, you know. When we went to see the rats yesterday and you said how tame they were, and he must be handling them loads—"

"But he isn't," Becky interrupted. "He looked all embarrassed, I was watching him – that's why I said it, to see what he did."

"I know! But, don't you see, he didn't go, 'Oh no, I never let them out of the cage', did he? He just kind of let it go. He didn't say anything."

Katie nodded. "She's right, Becky. He didn't want to admit he wasn't looking after them properly in front of us all. Maybe you *can* shame him into looking after them. It won't be easy, though."

Annabel looked over at Jack. "So you're going to try and charm him into doing what you want?"

Becky blushed again. "Suppose so."

"Excellent! Can we watch?" Annabel gave her sister a teasing smile.

"No way. You'll just try and make me laugh, I know you will. You're staying well out of it."

"Awww. That's not fair, it was my magazine that gave you the idea."

"No. I'm not going to do it now anyway, I need to think about it. And I can't exactly walk up to him and start trying out tricks from magazines with all of you watching, that'll make it really obvious."

And she sounded so definite that Annabel had to be content with that.

As it turned out, Becky got the ideal opportunity in science that afternoon. They were supposed to be doing some weird experiment that involved boiling water and putting it in beakers wrapped up in fleecy stuff. Somehow this was meant to tell you something about penguins in the Antarctic keeping themselves warm.

Normally penguins would have made Becky much more interested in whatever they were doing – she loved them. But today she was more interested in Jack and Robin being at the next Bunsen burner. All they had to do for the experiment was record the temperature of the water every minute, so she had plenty of time for chatting as long as she was careful. Mrs Stafford, their science teacher, was quite nice, and as long as they were quiet when she was talking she didn't mind a bit of noise.

"Jack?" Becky asked, in a slightly quavery voice, aware that Fran was glued to every word, and glad that Katie and Annabel were a couple of benches back this time.

"Yeah?" Jack looked round enquiringly.

Becky smiled at him. "Just wondering how the rats were."

"Oh they're fine," Jack said, a bit dismissively.

"We were so impressed when we saw them. Weren't we?" She nudged Fran, who nodded. "I mean, even though they're not pets, you're still looking after them really well – you must be, they're so tame and lovely, and they wouldn't be so friendly if you didn't play with them all the time."

Jack gazed down at his list of temperatures, looking a bit embarrassed. "Mmmm," he said, and then turned to Robin. "It's time again."

Becky pretended to take Jack's sudden interest in the accuracy of his experiment results at face value, and went back to her own beaker, grinning at Fran.

"Excellent! If we keep doing that whenever we get the chance, it's got to make him feel bad when he looks at One and Two," said Fran. "He'll feel guilty when he sees them looking all lonely, and he'll take them out and give them some attention, I'm sure he will."

Becky sighed. "Either that or he'll just cover the cage in a blanket so he can't see them at all. But I reckon it's got to be worth a try. We mustn't be too obvious though."

Unfortunately she didn't realize that her

plan was already attracting attention. Not only had Annabel and Katie and the others been desperately trying (and failing) to hear what was going on, but Amy and Cara were right behind her and Fran, and they *had* heard.

Amy had spent the last couple of days looking for a way to get back at David Morley *and* Becky for the way David had spoken to her in history on Tuesday. She was happy to bide her time, but neither of them were going to get away with it. She hid Becky's sudden interest in Jack away in her mental stash of "possibly useful information", and tapped her pen against her teeth thoughtfully. She was looking at Max Cooper – the one other person she knew who really couldn't stand the triplets. She'd heard about the way he'd upset Becky in the dining hall, and everyone in the school had heard about his deliberate foul on Katie in the football match (Amy totally approved, but thought he was stupid to have been so obvious). Perhaps now they could work together? She needed a plan. . .

Annabel bounced up to Becky at the end of the lesson. "Do you think it worked?"

"I don't know. I think I'm going to have to keep on doing it a bit at a time," Becky mused.

"Like Chinese water torture," put in Katie cheerfully.

"That's not very nice!" said Becky in a slightly shocked voice. "But yes, I s'pose so."

And that's what she did. Dripping away at Jack, whenever she and Fran had a good opportunity. They dropped in plenty of nice things about lizards too – as Becky said to Fran when she was over at her house that weekend, helping her give Feathers a much-needed bath, if they could make him think about rats and lizards at the same time, maybe he'd start to like the rats more.

By Monday, Amy had seen Becky talking to Jack enough times that she thought it was worth saying something – something that would really get to her. She wasn't quite sure what was going on – whether Becky liked Jack and was just using these stupid rats as an excuse, or what – but she knew that Becky would be horribly embarrassed either way.

It was cold and wet, so at lunch everyone was gathered in the classroom, sitting on the tables, reading, chatting or playing a bizarre game of volleyball with someone's rolled-up scarf.

The triplets and their friends were sitting together as usual, having about five conversations at once, and ducking every time the scarf went over. Across on the other side of the classroom, Amy, Cara and Emily had their heads together, and every so often mean little giggles issued from their corner. The triplets exchanged frowns. This could be bad news. Amy was fairly nasty to most of their year, except when she wanted something, but she particularly liked to get at the triplets' group – they reckoned it was because she was jealous. Amy liked to be the centre of attention, and she couldn't cope with the triplets being more popular than she was – especially when they didn't even seem to care that much.

They were right to suspect trouble. A couple of minutes later, Amy was leading the way across the room, a studiously innocent expression on her face. She was followed by Cara and Emily, both smirking.

Amy plumped herself down on the empty table next to them, and cooed sweetly, "Hi Becky!"

Becky actually looked over her shoulder. She knew perfectly well that there was no one else in the class called Becky, but she was so desperate for Amy to be talking to someone else behind her. But of course Amy wasn't.

"We were wondering. . ." Amy giggled charmingly, and exchanged looks with Cara and Emily. "Are you actually going out with Jack now? Or hasn't he asked you yet?"

"Wh-what?" Becky whispered, casting panicked looks at Katie and Annabel.

"You could always ask him, you know — if you don't want to wait. It's OK for a girl to ask a boy out."

"Especially if they're desperate," sniggered Emily.

"Which you do seem to be, Becky," — another charming smile from Amy — "I mean, you're always hanging around him."

Cara nodded. "Everyone's noticed, Becky."

"Shut up!" Katie snapped furiously. Amy, Emily and Cara had been swapping remarks so quickly that this was the first opportunity she'd had to break in. "What's it got to do with you anyway?"

"I don't want to go out with Jack!" Becky gasped, finally getting the words out.

"Yeah, it really looks like it," smiled Amy. "Anyway, we just wanted to wish you luck. I'm not quite sure what you see in him, of course, but then I suppose you can't be too picky."

Amy cast her sparkly smile over the whole group, and the three of them waltzed off, sniggering.

Annabel put her arm round Becky, who was doing a goldfish impression, bug-eyed and gaping, as she tried to gather her wits. "Ignore her. She's probably just jealous."

"Yeah." Katie nodded vigorously. "Don't worry about it, Becky. She's an idiot."

The others nodded, and murmured soothing things about how crazy and mean Amy was, and how Becky should forget her.

But it wasn't exactly easy to do. Did everyone in the class think she was chasing after Jack? Did Jack think so? She had been using tricks from a magazine that were supposed to get you a boyfriend, after all. Maybe it had been totally obvious to everyone! This was so embarrassing – she felt like she just wanted to curl up in a corner and die.

And unfortunately, it was all about to get much worse. . .

Chapter Seven

Becky watched miserably as Amy, Emily and Cara disappeared out of the classroom, looking back at her and giggling nastily. She sighed, her breath catching in her throat as she tried not to cry. Well, at least now they were gone – she had a bit of breathing space until the end of lunch.

Or so she thought. Unfortunately, Amy's master plan was just getting started. . .

As Becky stared at the tabletop, trying to believe the comforting things the others were saying, she heard Katie and Annabel's soothing nothings tail off. They weren't out of patience with her already, were they? She looked up. Her sisters were staring over to the other side of the classroom, their backs stiff and grim expressions on their faces.

"What is it?" she asked worriedly, sitting up, and looking in the same direction. Then her heart sank. The small group of girls by the window was chuckling over something, and as she watched, a couple of them looked straight at her, then ducked their heads down quickly, sniggering.

"What are they doing?" she asked the others, her voice rising panickily – Becky just couldn't believe that something else was going wrong.

"I don't know," said Katie. "But I'm going to find out." And she got up and stalked over to the group, looking murderous.

"Come on," said Annabel firmly. "We need to know what's going on." And she tugged Becky up from her chair and propelled her in Katie's wake. Fran, Saima and Megan followed – it didn't look like Katie needed the moral support, but Becky certainly did. As Fran got up, she noticed Max watching avidly.

Now, why was he so interested? She kept an eye on him as she went after the others.

Katie was standing with her arms folded, staring down at the group of girls, who were looking uncomfortable.

"Why were you looking at my sister like that?" she demanded.

"We didn't mean anything. . ." said Janie Holmes – she wasn't someone the triplets knew well, but she'd always seemed perfectly nice. "It's just – someone gave us this." She took a piece of paper from one of the others, and passed it to Katie, casting an apologetic glance at Becky as she did so.

Katie read what was written on it, then crumpled the note up furiously.

"Sorry!" said Janie – Katie's face was so thunderous, she felt she needed to apologize.

Katie just scowled and herded the others in front of her out of the classroom.

"What is it? Where are we going?" Annabel hissed at her, but Katie just snapped. "Come on!" and marched out into the corridor.

They gathered a little way along, where there was a big window sill to sit on, and squashed on to it.

Becky stared very determinedly at Katie, and held out her hand. "Give me the note. Oh, come on, Katie, I have to know what it says!"

Katie didn't really want to, because she knew it would really upset her, but Becky looked as though she meant it, so reluctantly she passed it to her. Annabel and the others looked over Becky's shoulder as she read:

Don't talk to that cheat Becky Ryan – she's two-timing David and Jack!

Becky stared down at it – how could anyone say that? She wasn't going out with either of them, let alone both!

"Who wrote this?" demanded Annabel, snatching it out of her hand. "I'm going to kill them!"

Suddenly Fran jumped down from the window sill. "He did!" she snapped. "Oh, come on, do you even need to ask?" She waved a hand dramatically down the corridor to where a very familiar face had just popped back round their classroom door.

"Max!" snarled Katie and Annabel together, and they grabbed Becky and stormed back into the classroom. Max was sitting at a table on his own, apparently transfixed by the game he was playing on his phone.

"Did you send that note round?" Annabel spat at him.

Max just looked back at her, his face innocently confused. "Oh, hello, Katie – where's your *mummy*?"

"Oh, of course he did!" said Fran disgustedly. "He's just not brave enough to admit it, that's all. Loser!"

As she'd expected, that got Max talking. "So what if I did? It's only the truth. People have a right to know." He smirked. "After all, she might start flirting with someone else. I'm just warning people what kind of a person *sweet* little Becky really is!"

Becky gasped in horror. This just couldn't be happening.

"You moron! You're talking complete garbage – Becky and David are mates, that's all!" Annabel said scathingly.

"And she's only been talking to Jack about his rats, she's not chasing after him!" Katie snapped.

"That's not what Jack thinks!" snarled Max – he was standing by now, and practically spitting in their faces. Over the other side of the classroom, Jack was looking completely gobsmacked at this news, and his mate Robin was nearly having hysterics.

"That's so typical – as soon as a girl speaks to a boy you assume she fancies him!" Annabel conveniently forgot that this was what her magazine had been suggesting all along, as she scowled at all three boys.

Max shook his head sadly. "Well, you only need to look at her – if I'm so wrong, why's she looking so guilty? She knows she's messed them around. David's really annoyed with her." He folded his arms and gazed triumphantly at Becky's dismayed face.

He didn't get the chance for long. Becky returned his stare for all of three seconds before the pressure of everyone (because quite a lot of the rest of the class were now blatantly listening in) staring at her became way too much. She shoved herself past Max harder than she would ever dare to normally, and raced out of the classroom.

Katie and Annabel stayed only to hiss, "You're not getting away with this!" and "Brain-dead moron!" respectively at Max before they shot out after her.

Fran, Megan and Saima just glared at Max, but he seemed totally unfazed, and smiled sweetly as he walked away.

Megan voiced what the other two had been

thinking. "It's silly, isn't it? When something like this happens, you don't know whether they want us there or not. It's not like being friends with just one person."

Saima nodded and Fran made a face. "I know – I mean if Becky wasn't a triplet I'd have gone after her straight away, but I kind of think it's better to leave it as just them for a bit."

Meanwhile, Katie and Annabel were trying to work out where Becky had gone. They tried three sets of girls' toilets, which all seemed to be occupied by gangs of older girls who stared at them in disgust.

Katie slammed the door of the last set of loos angrily. "Where *is* she? I'm going to kill him, I really am!"

Annabel nodded. "But once we've sorted Becky out, I want to know what's really happening. What's she playing at? I hate to say it, but that idiot's right, there is *something* going on, or she wouldn't have run off like that."

Katie looked confused. "Do you think so? I thought she was just upset because Max was being so mean – you don't think she actually has been doing what he said, playing them against each other?"

"No, of course not!" Annabel replied scornfully. "Don't be an idiot, Katie. Can you imagine Becky doing that?"

"Well then—"

"What I mean is, I think maybe she does like David and she's upset because she thinks she's hurt his feelings. And maybe she's worried he won't like her any more," Annabel added practically.

"When you say like—" Katie paused.

"Mmmm?" said Annabel, who was looking around the corridor as if in search of inspiration. Where would Becky have gone?

"When you say like, do you mean *like* like, or just like?"

Amazingly, Annabel understood what she

meant perfectly. "Don't know. That's what I want to ask Becky. I reckon she must have gone outside."

"You think?" Katie asked doubtfully, looking out of the window at the drizzling rain. "I suppose she might have done, if she really wanted to get away from people." Suddenly she grabbed Annabel's arm. "The tree! I bet she's on the other side of the tree!" And she raced out of the door, heading for the chestnut tree where the triplets often gathered with their friends before school – it was huge, and Becky could quite easily be round the side by the wall, hidden from them.

Meanwhile, Becky *was* on the other side of the tree, and she'd heard her sisters coming. But she wasn't really sure whether or not she wanted them to find her. At the same time as she was desperate for Katie and Annabel to give her a hug and tell her that everything was going to be OK, she was dreading the questions they were bound to ask. Especially Annabel, who was so into boys and relationships.

The real problem was, she'd been asking herself all the questions already, and she had absolutely no idea what the answers were. At least she knew that what Max and Amy had said was completely untrue. She'd quite liked Jack, until she'd found out about the rats, but she had absolutely no interest in going out with him. That didn't mean she wanted to go out with David either, though. She just thought he was − *nice*. But she knew that Annabel was going to get madly excited if she admitted that. She didn't even know if Max had been making it all up! Perhaps David hadn't even noticed she'd been talking to Jack. Really, why should he? He probably couldn't care less. How was she supposed to know?

She could hear Katie's racing footsteps now, and she rubbed a hand across her eyes to try and make herself look a bit less of a state. It didn't do much good. She'd been properly crying in the hiccupping, heaving, streaming fashion for a good five minutes, and what she needed was an industrial-sized pack of tissues and some eyedrops, not the back of her hand.

"Oh, *Becky*!" Katie flung herself down on a tree root next to her sister. "Look at you! You muppet, what did you run off for?" She dug a crumpled but basically clean tissue out of her pocket, and handed it to her sister. Meanwhile, Annabel panted up, and then stood with her hands on her hips glaring at Becky. She was about to tell Becky off for being a total idiot, and getting her wet so her hair would probably go all frizzy, but then she looked at her properly and realized that this just wasn't the time. She sat down next to the pair of them, and then stood up again to go through her pockets for anything useful. Unfortunately, all she had was cherry lipgloss, and even Annabel could see that shiny, nice-tasting lips were pretty low on Becky's list of priorities right now.

"Don't you even have a tissue?" asked Katie hopefully.

"Nope. Well, I do, but they're in my bag, which is, let me see, not here, in the middle of the playground, where it's *raining*. Can we go in, pleeease?"

"Can't – go – anywhere looking – like this," heaved Becky.

"Well, you're not going to stop looking like that until we sort you out, and we can't do that here, with one tissue," pointed out Annabel reasonably. She held out a hand to pull Becky up, and reluctantly Becky grabbed it. Then the three of them headed back into school, to find the least-occupied of the three sets of toilets that Katie and Annabel had just done a whistle-stop tour of.

Luckily, when Annabel poked her nose round the door of the first lot, the Year Tens seemed to have gone. Becky'd mostly stopped crying anyway, so it was more TLC she needed than tissues. Finally, Annabel reckoned she was in a fit state for the third degree, and ignoring Katie's frowns, she met Becky's eyes where she was gazing at her reflection in the mirror.

Becky looked away, and pretended to be very interested in washing her hands, but Annabel wasn't having that.

"Becky, you have to tell us what's going on, you know."

Becky looked back at her sister's reflection. It was slightly easier to face down a glass version of Annabel than the real thing, but not much. "I don't *have* to tell you anything, actually," she said, feeling miffed. Why did Annabel assume that every detail of Becky's life was there for her and Katie to discuss? Then her common sense kicked in with the answer – because it always had been, of course. The triplets, even though they were as different in personality as they were identical to look at, were also very, very close.

Becky sighed, and then turned to face the

real Annabel, and Katie too. She gave a small smile – it was about all she could manage. "Anyway, I can't tell you what's going on, 'cause I don't know. Don't look at me like that!" she protested, seeing their disbelieving faces. "Really I don't. I was sitting there trying to work it out."

"But do you *like* him?" demanded Annabel, refusing to let this slip through her fingers.

"Who, Jack?"

"No, David, you idiot! Of course David!"

"Well, yes, but—" Becky caught Annabel's gleeful glance at Katie. "*But*, Bel, I don't know whether I like him that way, or just as a friend, or what. And I haven't a clue what he thinks about me. So it doesn't make any difference whether I do or not."

"Of course it does!" Annabel exploded. "What are you talking about? If you like him then we find that sort of thing out! How useless can you be?" She softened this last comment with a hug – she adored Becky, but sometimes she could be really feeble! "This is so exciting! You could end up going out with him – I can't believe you're going to be the first one of us with a boyfriend!"

Katie was looking blank. Like Annabel, she'd always assumed that her popular, outgoing, fashionable sister would be going out with boys first. That it should be Becky came as a big shock. She could cope with the idea of *Bel* and boys – but now she was feeling rather left out, and confused.

"Stop it!" said Becky urgently. "Look Bel, just go back about ten steps, OK? I *knew* this would happen! He isn't going to be my boyfriend, Katie, so stop looking at me as though I've grown fur or something. We'll just forget it – ignore it, and everyone else will stop bothering about it too."

"Yeah, right!" laughed Annabel. "No way, Becky. You can't do that. Even if Max was lying and David doesn't know about all this, someone's bound to tell him what Max and Amy said. You can't just pretend it never happened."

Becky looked like she might start to cry again, and Annabel softened her voice. "Look, it's OK, honestly. You've got us to help you, and the others, we'll find out what's going on." Annabel carefully glossed over the fact that Katie was looking as though she didn't want to have anything to do with this plan, and scowled at her. "*Won't we*?"

"I suppose," Katie agreed, very hesitantly, for her. "If that's what you want, Becky," she added doubtfully.

"But I don't *know* what I want!" Becky wailed.

Annabel was about to launch into an impassioned explanation of how this was complete nonsense and they couldn't just do nothing, when the bell went. Becky wasn't sure whether she was glad or not — at least in lessons Annabel couldn't keep going on at her about David (much) but now she had to go back into class and face everybody staring, which was going to be just as bad. . .

Chapter Eight

Meanwhile, Annabel was absolutely right. David hadn't been in the classroom when Amy and then Max were mouthing off, but someone *had* told him what was going on — and it was about the worst possible person.

Max lost no time when he saw David come in with Jordan and Matthew.

"Hear that Becky Ryan made you look a bit stupid," he said, smirking.

David looked nonplussed. He got on all right with Max normally — he'd been pretty disgusted with him after he'd attacked Katie though. "What?" he asked warily.

"Becky — she's been making a play for Jack, you know, as well as you. You should do something about it, mate, you shouldn't just let her get away with it."

"I don't know what you're talking about. . ." David stammered.

"Oh, I think you do," Max snarled nastily. "You've been two-timed. Everyone knows, they're all laughing at you."

David looked round worriedly, and several people did seem to be staring at them.

Max gave a mean snigger as he walked away – he could tell he'd really got to David, even though David hadn't seemed to know what he was on about. Maybe Amy's information was wrong? But it didn't really matter anyway – the point was to upset the triplets as much as possible, and they'd certainly managed that.

The triplets raced back into the classroom to get their stuff ready, Becky carefully avoiding looking at anyone, except to give Fran a quick smile. She didn't know what kind of comments she was going to have to put up with from everybody, but she certainly wasn't going to give people a chance by catching anyone's eye. She managed to keep this up for the rest of the day, staring at her books and doing her best to pretend that she wasn't actually there.

It was harder to zone out the interested muttering that she could hear every so often from some of the girls, though – comments along the lines of "Did she *really*?" and "So what did *he* say?" Everyone seemed fascinated, but Katie and Annabel were doing very well at giving the impression that anybody who dared to mention boys to Becky might be frozen by a combined icy glare, and the triplets and their friends moved from lesson to lesson in a protective block.

On the way home, though, Becky was in a state again. All afternoon Jack had avoided looking at her – and more to the point, so had David. But they were the only ones who had, and Amy and Max's gleeful grins, together with the constant whispering from the rest of the class, had made her feel sick.

"Everyone's talking about it! It's so horrible – they think *I'm* horrible – I don't know what to do." She turned hopefully to Katie. "Do you think Mum would let me stay off school tomorrow?"

"Well, for a start, *no*. And do you actually want Amy and Max going round school tomorrow smirking because they think they've got to you?"

"They have got to me!"

"That's not the point, Becky," put in Annabel. "People'll just gossip more if you're not at school – it's a bad idea, honestly."

Fran and Saima, who were walking home with them, nodded seriously, and Becky's shoulders slumped again.

"I just hate it when I can feel people are talking about me," she said miserably.

Annabel grinned at her. "Becky, most of the girls in the class are probably jealous! They'd

115

love to be the centre of attention like this. You've got to go back to school tomorrow and act like you couldn't care less. Like you think it's funny."

Becky whirled round. "Bel! It's *not* funny. I hate it. Amy and Max are laughing their heads off, Jack's never going to speak to me again and David – " She stopped, and Annabel looked at her with interest – so did Fran and Saima.

"David what?" enquired Annabel, looking at Becky's red face and practically purring. "You *do* like him!"

"David might really be upset, is all I was going to say," Becky muttered.

"So what are you going to do?" asked Saima excitedly.

"Are you going to talk to him about it?" Fran suggested.

"No!" Becky exclaimed in horror.

Katie looked almost relieved, but Annabel was positively affronted. "You have to! You can't just leave it like that. Besides," she added cunningly, "you've got to speak to him. He's going to be wondering what's going on – you can't just leave him like that, it's mean."

Becky sighed. Annabel was right – although she knew perfectly well her sister was being sneaky, she couldn't just let David stew over the whole thing. But it was going to be so embarrassing! How could she go up to him and basically ask if he'd mind telling her if he fancied her or not, because everyone was gossiping about it?

"You could even ask him out! I'm sure he does like you!"

Becky shuddered at the idea, and Annabel looked at her impatiently. How could Becky not be as desperate as she was to know what was going on? She wanted all the juicy details, and unless Becky had a personality transplant in the next day or so, she was not likely to get them. She sighed crossly. And then she had an idea. "Why don't you let *me* talk to him?"

"You can't do that!" exclaimed Katie.

"Why not? Becky wants to know whether David likes her. Don't you?" Annabel nudged Becky, and Katie, Saima and Fran all stared at her expectantly.

"I – I suppose so," Becky murmured.

Katie made a huffing noise, and Annabel glared at her. "Just because you aren't interested in going out with somebody, it doesn't mean Becky can't!" she snapped.

"Oh, I suppose not." Katie shrugged. "It seems so silly, though. If Becky likes him, why can't *she* talk to him?"

"Excuse me, I am here, you know!" Becky put in irritably.

Katie and Annabel both looked at her apologetically.

"Sorry Becky," soothed Annabel, then she turned back to Katie. "But really, can you imagine Becky trying to talk to David about all this? It would be torture. For both of them probably. It would be much easier if they had a go-between, and I've offered, so I don't see what the problem is. All I'm going to do is find out if he likes her or not, then Becky can take it from there. Can't you?" She whisked round to Becky at this point, and pinned her with a "do as you're told" stare. Becky nodded mutely.

Katie just shrugged. She thought the whole thing was mad, but if they wanted to – well, it wasn't up to her, it was up to Becky. She was just a bit worried that Annabel was taking over for her, and pushing Becky further than she really wanted to go. "So you're going to talk to David tomorrow?" she asked Annabel.

Becky made a frightened kind of noise – this all seemed to be going way too fast. What if David said he wasn't interested at all? She'd die. But Annabel nodded determinedly at Katie.

Katie frowned back worriedly. "Well, OK – but you need to tell us *every word*."

"Excellent," said Annabel, satisfied. "Tomorrow at break?"

She was asking Becky, but Becky had a strong feeling that it wasn't really up to her any more. She nodded anyway. Annabel in go-ahead mode was hard to say no to – and this *was* what she wanted, wasn't it?

Next morning, after Becky had spent a worried evening at home avoiding Annabel, who kept trying to show her clothes that would be good to wear on her first date with David, and then woken up about three times in the night after weird dreams involving going on a date with a giant rat, she ran into another problem.

The triplets walked into the classroom for registration, and were met by a spooky hush. Annabel and Katie breezed on in, ignoring the sudden silence completely, but Becky's cheeks flamed as she desperately tried to avoid all the interested looks.

Amy and her lot were giggling and pointing, and Max was smirking. David appeared to be staring out of the window and not looking at her at all, luckily – where was Jack? She caught him staring at her speculatively when he thought she wasn't looking, and then he blushed redder than she had as he realized she'd noticed. It was so funny that she grinned, and he turned quickly back to his mates and started talking very fast.

The grin seemed to make Becky feel better – *how* silly were all those girls who were staring? Didn't they have anything better to do? But her sudden lift in spirits didn't last long. Jack was so nervous that he was talking too loud, and as Becky sat down she caught some of his conversation with his friend Ben.

"Nope. I don't reckon it's happening. I've had them weeks, and Two's not even fat – what's the point of keeping the things if they're not going to have any babies? I'm just going to give up and cut my losses."

Becky and Fran exchanged horrified looks. Cut his losses? Did that mean One and Two were heading for the snake shop? Would Jack do that? Watching his sulky face, Becky decided that of course he would. Now what was she going to do?

At least panicking about the rats' future gave her less time for obsessing about what was going to happen at break. Annabel's excited wriggling and constant conspiratorial glances were a bit of a problem, though. She was obviously looking forward to this enormously. Becky spent the small amount of time that she could spare from worrying about those poor rats worrying that she was really weird somehow. Why was it Annabel who was so keen on all of this, and not her? Shouldn't she be excited, being about to find out whether David liked her? And actually, although she thought David was really nice, and very sweet and funny, all she felt was horribly nervous that he was going to catch her and Katie spying on them. She shuddered. How embarrassing would *that* be. . .

The double lesson before break seemed to race past, and Annabel led the others back to their classroom to dump their bags.

"What do we do now?" Becky asked anxiously.

"Absolutely *nothing*, that's the whole point!" said Annabel, very firmly. "Just find somewhere you can watch, and stay out of my way!"

Katie and Becky and the others decided to stay in the corridor and watch from one of the big window sills. The last thing they wanted was for Amy and her little gang to see them following Annabel around, and demand to know why they were lurking in that suspicious way. They'd just have to trust Annabel to report back.

Annabel's plan was pretty simple. Once she'd spotted David (reading a football magazine on the steps with Kieran, another boy from their class) she approached the boys with her sweetest smile.

"David?"

David looked up, confused. Obviously this was one of the triplets, but it wasn't Becky, as he'd thought for a split-second. It was Annabel, who didn't really talk to him much – he'd had a couple of good football conversations with Katie, but Annabel was a bit girly – he didn't feel like he had much in common with her. "Er, hi. . ." he managed, at last. After the stuff Max had said yesterday, he didn't really know how to react to her.

Annabel's high-power charm smile was still in place, and Kieran was starting to look as though he might spontaneously combust.

"Can I talk to you in private?"

David wasn't immune to the smile either, and he got up and trotted after her, without asking why. Annabel took him over to the chestnut tree where the triplets often sat, as it was fairly quiet there.

"I wanted to talk to you about Becky," she said seriously.

David managed to look excited, embarrassed and terrified at the same time. It was quite impressive, Annabel thought, especially when you considered how much of his face was covered up by that irritatingly too-long hair. She turned up the wattage on the smile.

"She's really upset about this whole thing with Max. He's been spreading these horrible rumours, telling everyone that she's chasing after you and Jack and being really cruel to you." She paused, but David unhelpfully didn't say anything. "I'm sorry if this is the first you've heard of it, but we thought you ought to know it just isn't true – Becky's only been talking to Jack because he's got these two pet rats and she's worried about them. He wanted to breed baby rats for snakes to eat, and she hated it, so she's been trying to stop him."

David got as far as an enquiring eyebrow.

Annabel continued, although admittedly the smile was starting to look very slightly strained. David was tough.

"So when Max had a go at her" – Annabel was encouraged to see David stiffen up here, and decided to pile on the sympathy plea – "she was really devastated. She didn't want you to think she was doing what he said. Which is why I'm talking to you. And we wondered if anything Max said was true – you know, whether you actually were upset because you like Becky, or if he just made all that up?"

She looked at him hopefully. David looked deeply embarrassed, and peered worriedly at Annabel from under his fringe. Was this all some elaborate plot to make him look really, really stupid? Then he decided he didn't care – he might think Annabel was a bit too girly, but she was so similar to Becky, and Becky he liked a lot. So he chose to trust her and go for it.

"Yes."

Annabel managed a controlled squawk. "Yes, he made it up?!"

"No, no, sorry. I mean yes, I do like her. She's really sweet. And very pretty. You, er, all are.

I never said anything to Max about it, but it's true." Then he appeared to be struck dumb, and just stared over her head at one particular leaf as though it was the most amazing thing he'd ever seen.

Annabel took a deep breath, and smiled widely at him. Finally! How difficult could it be to get a straight answer? "Thanks, David. I'll tell her."

She watched, giggling, as David shot off to the other side of the playground as though the leaf had suddenly grown fangs. Then she bolted – she had to go and tell Becky!

Chapter Nine

Annabel thought that the whole situation with David was simple now. She just had to tell Becky what he'd said, Becky would go and talk to him in an "I like you too, please ask me out" kind of way, he would, and everything would be sorted.

She'd reckoned without Becky. Admittedly her sister's first reaction was all she could have hoped for – Becky was practically fainting with excitement, and squeaking disjointed things like, "Are you sure?" and "Did he really—?" and "It's so exciting!" But she didn't carry on to the obvious next step – what do we do now? When Saima asked that very question, Becky just looked blank.

Annabel stared at her, gimlet-eyed. "You are *going* to talk to him, aren't you?" she asked, her tone of voice strongly suggesting that the answer no would get Becky disembowelled with a compass.

"You can't just not do anything!" Saima assured Becky, in a shocked way. "That would be awful."

"It would be cruel," Annabel declared firmly. "Like torturing a dog — I can see why you compared him to an Old English Sheepdog, Becky, he's got puppydog eyes."

Becky hung her head. Annabel's force of character had carried her through to this point, and now she didn't know *what* to do. She realized that her misgivings about the whole plan had been right all along. It was unfair to have let Annabel get David's hopes up, if she wasn't going to follow through. She looked sideways under her lashes at Katie, who'd been silent up till now, hoping for some back-up. But Katie was standing with her arms folded, glaring at her. In fact, she and Annabel were like cross china dogs at either end of a mantelpiece – except that she didn't think that their glares meant the same thing at all. Katie clearly thought the whole thing was mad, and wanted her to stop it now.

"I need to think about it," said Becky, conjuring a firm voice from somewhere she hadn't known she'd got. "Honestly, Bel. Maybe I'll talk to him tomorrow." And luckily, the bell rang just then, and Becky could escape back into school. . .

She held out for the rest of the day, despite Annabel's battery of looks, which ranged from pleading to full–on threatening, and practically everything in between. She also had to avoid looking at David, which was more difficult.

In fact, the only thing she could do was focus on her "save the rats" campaign, which was clearly getting more urgent. At lunch, she and Fran held a council of war.

"Do you think he is going to sell One and

Two?" asked Fran, nibbling on a chip in very rat-like fashion.

"Definitely," said Becky. "They're no use any more, are they? We can't let it happen."

Fran went on to her chocolate pudding, and consumed a few mouthfuls, quietly. Then suddenly she looked up in excitement, as though the sugar had kicked in and sent some energy to her brain. "Look, Becky, if all Jack wants is money, why don't we just give it to him?"

It only took Becky a few seconds to see what she meant. "You mean, buy his rats? Fran, that's a brilliant idea! I mean, I bet I can offer him more than the exotic pet shop would, and I could buy his cage as well – they wouldn't want that. You star!" She beamed delightedly at her friend, and wondered how she could have been so stupid – it was the obvious answer.

Becky was desperate to get home that afternoon to talk to Mum about the rats. Katie and Megan were playing in a football match after school, so Becky and Fran walked home with Annabel and Saima, both of whom spent the entire walk looking sorrowfully at Becky, and sighing exasperatedly at every mention of rats. They clearly couldn't believe that Becky wasn't analysing every second of the conversation with David, and planning her next move with precision. And Annabel was fairly disgusted at the idea of Jack's rats actually becoming part of her household.

"Becky! Haven't you got *enough* animals? Four guinea pigs and two cats? Do you think Mum's going to let you?"

Becky grimaced. "I don't know. I hope so. I mean, when I tell her what'll happen to them otherwise, I think she will. We'll have to see."

"Can't we talk about what's happening with David for a bit now?" pleaded Annabel. "I can't believe you're just ignoring it!"

"I'm not ignoring it," snapped Becky crossly, sick of being pressured. "I'm *thinking* about it, that's all. You'll just have to wait. I've got more important things to worry about anyway."

Annabel gaped. "Those rats? More important. . ." She tailed off, speechless, and spent the rest of the walk home stalking ahead with Saima, muttering evilly.

The triplets' mum had finished work for the day and was starting to make their tea for when Katie got back. She'd put out a plate of biscuits for Becky and Annabel in the meantime.

Becky and Fran had been trying to work out a mother-persuading strategy on the way home, while desperately trying to ignore Annabel and Saima, but the problem was time. Becky was fairly sure she could have got her mum to agree to rats for Christmas (she'd already got her started thinking about the idea), but that would have been a slow-build campaign – and now this had to become an all-out assault, and it wasn't Becky's normal way of doing things. Still, she did have the advantage of her mum's soft heart, and the terrible fate that awaited One and Two if she didn't rescue them. Fran was annoyed that she couldn't try and buy them herself – Becky wouldn't have minded, it had been Fran's idea, and she'd still get to play with them – but she was sure her dad was a harder sell, especially when he was feeling anti-pet anyway.

Annabel sat down at the table and took a biscuit. She bit into it savagely, and scowled at Becky. Becky just sighed. It was clear that there was no use expecting any help from *her* – though considering Annabel's feelings about rats, that would have been pretty optimistic anyway,

"Mum?"

"Yes, darling?" Mrs Ryan looked round from the chicken stew she was making. It was looking very watery, and she was wondering if she'd misread the recipe.

"There's a boy at school, Jack, he came to our party, do you remember?"

Her mother looked doubtful. "Maybe. . ."

"Well, it doesn't matter, but it was his house we went to on Wednesday, to see his pet rats."

"Mmm."

"Only they aren't really pets. . . Are you listening?" Becky added suspiciously. Mum looked very preoccupied with dinner.

"Yes, sorry, love, I was just thinking we might have to eat this out of bowls. Go on, keep talking." And Mrs Ryan put a lid on the pan, and came to sit next to Annabel, opposite Becky.

"He was wanting to breed them – to sell to the exotic pet shop in Stallford as *snake food*!" Becky said the last part of this in an impressive hiss, hoping to make her mother see what an awful idea it was.

Mrs Ryan grimaced. "Oh dear."

Oh dear? Was that *it*? Becky glared at her mother for a moment, and then realized that getting cross was not going to help.

"But his plan isn't going to work, because

actually he got tricked by the boy who sold him the rats, and they aren't a pair, they're both girls. So now he's getting impatient 'cause they haven't had babies, and I think he's going to sell the two he's got to the pet shop anyway. They're going to get eaten, Mum!"

Mrs Ryan was looking as though she could see that was not good, but she wasn't making the vital leap that Becky needed. She was going to have to spell it out.

"So I was thinking, could I buy his rats off him? I've got enough money, I think." Becky looked hopefully at her mother.

Mrs Ryan seemed doubtful. "Oh, Becky, are you sure? I mean, you've got so many pets to look after already. The time—"

"But you were going to think about me having them for Christmas, weren't you? This is just earlier, that's all. And those rats are going to die, Mum!"

"Well, I suppose so. I'm just worried how

they're going to fit in the shed – it's quite full of guinea pigs."

"The shed?" Becky looked blank. "Oh, Mum, no, the rats couldn't live in the shed. They're used to living in a house – it'd be too cold for them out there. They're indoor pets. They're going to live on the big window sill in our bedroom."

At this, Annabel, who'd been nibbling her way through the biscuits, wishing Becky would concentrate on the much more important issue of David, and only half-listening, sat bolt upright. "What?" she squeaked in horror. "You mean they're going to be in the *house*!"

"Well, yes. of course they are!"

"No *way*," squawked Annabel, at the same time as her mother said, "Oh Becky, I'm not sure. . ." Annabel won on volume and continued, "You can't put rats in our bedroom! That's disgusting! I'm not sleeping with those horrible things and that's final!"

"It's not up to you!" Becky snapped back

angrily. Wanting to defend the rats had fired her up – normally she hated arguments – but her mother stopped her.

"I'm sorry, Becky, but it's Bel's room too – and she really doesn't like rats. It's not fair to make her live in the same room with them, you have to see that. I'm really sorry, I know you want to help the rats, but I just don't think it's going to work out."

Becky was gobsmacked. It had all been sorted – and now it wasn't! How could Bel be so selfish? She shoved her chair back from the table and raced outside to the shed, already feeling tears at the back of her eyes.

Mrs Ryan sighed, and Annabel was left feeling defiant, and somehow a teensy bit guilty. This was so unfair! Becky couldn't expect her to share a room with nasty clawed biting things – Orlando was bad enough, but at least he always slept on Becky's bed. Rats would make the whole *room* smell horrible.

She didn't like upsetting Becky, though –

she and Katie bossed Becky around, but they always stood up for her as well. Annabel went upstairs to brood, and looked round at their room, beautifully ratless. She shuddered.

Becky still hadn't come out by the time Katie got home from her match, and Annabel wasted no time telling her other triplet about Becky's plan.

"In our room! Can you believe it? It would be awful!"

Katie shrugged, and nearly fell over, as she was changing into her jeans. "I don't think it would be that bad – they were quite sweet really, Bel."

"Not you too!" Annabel wailed. "They *smell*!"

"I think that's only if you don't clean them out properly. The guinea pigs don't smell, do they? And Jack's room didn't smell – much. Becky would keep them spotless anyway."

Annabel still looked mutinous, and Katie

shrugged again. "I'm going to talk to her. Mum wants me to get her to come in for tea."

Meanwhile Becky was curled in her favourite shed corner again, not even holding one of the guinea pigs. She felt like everything was about to fall on her head. The rats weren't going to be saved after all. She supposed Annabel wasn't just being unreasonable, she really did find them creepy. It was probably something she'd inherited from Dad, Becky thought bitterly. His reply to her excited email about rats had been very disappointing. He definitely wasn't a rat fan – apparently he just couldn't get over their "horrible bald pink tails". He wasn't trying to say she shouldn't have any, just that he wouldn't be playing with them.

The worst thing, though, was that she knew that Annabel and Saima were right – she had to make a decision about David soon, probably this evening. She realized sadly that she'd been focusing on the rats because it seemed like it was something fairly straightforward that she could solve – the thing with David was really complicated. Two tears dripped down her nose as she tried to work out what she wanted to do. She liked him so much – but did she want him to ask her out? What if it went all strange and embarrassing, and they couldn't even be friends any more? More tears joined the stream as she decided that they'd got past that stage already. If she didn't go and see him tomorrow about what he'd said to Annabel, he'd probably never talk to her again.

It was at that point that Katie arrived.

"Oh, Becky." She came and sat down next to her. "Look, maybe somebody else can buy Jack's rats. We'll sort it somehow."

"It's not just that," Becky sniffed. "David, as well."

Katie sighed. "Well, it's no use asking me. You've got to do that on your own."

A bigger sniff, then Becky whispered, "I do really like him. I'd hate it if we never hung around together."

"Then you'll have to go and talk to him tomorrow." Katie paused. And then she grinned. "Becky! I think I might just have solved your other problem too!"

"What?"

"What does Bel want most of all right now?"

"No rats," said Becky sadly.

"*More* than no rats!"

"Me to go and talk to David – oh!"

"Exactly. If you tell her that you're going to go and be nice to him so he'll ask you out, and that you want her to give you loads of advice, and do your hair and everything, then I reckon you might just be able to get her to live with the rats. . ."

Chapter Ten

Becky and Katie walked slowly up the garden path, planning. Their tea was on the table (Mrs Ryan had managed to solidify the stew a bit, so it was on plates), and Annabel was sitting waiting, looking mutinous. She was obviously expecting another argument from Becky, because she scowled at her when they came in. She was feeling guilty – she might hate the rats, but she didn't want to be responsible for getting them killed. But Becky managed a very small smile at her, which left Annabel feeling deeply confused, and even more guilty. Tea was a very silent meal, until halfway through the phone rang and Mrs Ryan got up to answer it – the triplets realized it was one of Mrs Ryan's friends, obviously wanting to settle in for a good long chat. Katie nudged Becky – this was the ideal time!

Becky put down her knife and fork, very carefully and neatly, licked her lips, and said, "Bel?"

Annabel's scowl returned – so Becky had just been waiting for Mum to go? Fine. She prepared for battle.

"I think you're right."

Annabel, who had had her mouth open to respond with a denunciation of all rodents, opened and shut it like a goldfish, then managed, "What?"

"About David. I'm going to do what you and Saima said, tomorrow. I'm going to go and talk to him." She noted Annabel's delighted face, and looked at Katie for further inspiration.

Katie put her head on one side, as though she'd just had an interesting idea. "You know,

Bel, if Becky's going to do what you want about David, maybe you ought to be more helpful about the rats?" she asked innocently.

Annabel returned to her goldfish look. Which was she more worried about — rats, or organizing her sister's love-life? The problem was, she just knew that if she left sorting things with David to Becky, she'd do it all *wrong*. She really needed Annabel's help, and it would be torture to watch it all go pear-shaped. . . How bad could rats really be?

"Maybe. . ." she muttered cautiously.

Becky leaped up from her chair and threw her arms round her sister. "Bel, you star! That's so nice of you!"

"I only said maybe!" Annabel answered in a strangulated yelp. "There's going to be conditions! Like . . . like if they start to smell they go straight to the snake shop! And you have to warn me when you're letting them out, so I can be somewhere else. Yes?"

"Definitely!" Becky nodded vigorously.

"Hmmm. Well, you have to give me some time to think of any more, OK?"

When Mrs Ryan came back into the room the atmosphere had got about ten degrees warmer, and Becky and Katie were giggling at something Annabel was drawing. She peered over at it – it appeared to be a plan of their bedroom.

"That" – Annabel stabbed with her red pen – "is the No Rat Zone, got it?"

"Mum!" squeaked Becky happily. "Bel's changed her mind! I can have the rats, if they never go anywhere near her stuff – it's excellent!"

"If I find one tiny little rat poo anywhere inside that red line. . ." Annabel warned.

"If I find one rat poo anywhere, full stop," agreed their mother.

"Rats are really clean," Becky assured them. "Honestly. You can even toilet train them. And I'll clean up if they have accidents, don't worry. They're going to have the most spotless, yummy-smelling cage you've ever seen. Oh, Mum, talking of cages, can I have a really good rat cage for Christmas? I can show you the kind I mean – I've got pictures from the net. Probably Mr Davies could order us one. Jack's just isn't big enough. And, um . . . can I have an advance on my pocket money to pay Jack?"

Mum sighed. "I suppose so. Sometimes I do wonder if it wouldn't be simpler to move to the zoo. And your dad's not going to be happy. He sent me a very panicky email about rats last week. Oh, don't look so worried, Becky – you'll just have to keep them out of his way."

Annabel suddenly looked up from her drawing. "Mum, can we have some people over on Saturday? If we invite Jack, he can bring the rats over, and Becky can show them to everyone."

"Well, yes, I suppose so." Mum looked

confused, Annabel seemed to have had a really remarkable change of heart.

She missed Annabel's wink as she said, "You can invite your friend David, Becky..."

After tea, the triplets went to do their homework. Annabel sat on the stairs (she swore it made it easier to think) and completed hers in record time. Then she raced up to their room, where Becky and Katie were working at the table. "Oh, come on, you must have finished!"

"No." Becky shook her head sadly. "I just can't get my head round this maths Mr Jones set us – all these angles and things." She gazed disgustedly at her maths exercise book. "And why am I ever going to want to *know* what the cosine of C is anyway? I don't mind maths when it's useful."

"Just pick some numbers – come on, I need to talk to you!" Annabel shoved Becky's pen into her hand.

Katie looked up from the geography she

was trying to learn. "Bel! Is that what you did? Mr Jones will kill you! And it's not fair – whenever you get into trouble the teachers always look at me, as though I should have stopped you. Go and get your book."

Annabel sighed dramatically. She supposed it was lucky that one of them was good at maths, but really, she couldn't care less tonight.

Twenty minutes later, Becky and Annabel had a vague idea of what was going on, and some answers that at least looked like they'd *thought* before they randomly picked some numbers, and Katie gave up – there was only so much trigonometry she could stuff into Annabel at the best of times, let alone now.

They cleared away their books, and curled up on Annabel's bed.

"So what's the plan, then?" asked Katie interestedly.

"*Well*," Annabel sat up straight and looked businesslike, "I think the best thing is for Becky to talk to David tomorrow, and invite him over on Saturday. That way you don't have to say anything embarrassing like 'please will you go out with me?' but it's still obvious you like him, do you see?"

Becky nodded seriously. If she was going to go through with this, she wanted it to be as unembarrassing as possible. "But I'm going to have to explain to him and Jack that Amy and Max made it all up – otherwise Jack won't even want to be in the same street with me, let alone the same house with me *and* David."

"Mmmm. Then we just have to get you looking irresistible on Saturday!"

"What?" squeaked Becky.

Annabel folded her arms firmly. "If *I* have to share a room with rodents, *you* are getting a makeover on Saturday morning, and don't even think of arguing."

Becky subsided – she could put up with Bel fussing over her, if it meant she got the rats. It took a lot of thinking about One and Two to get through the rest of the evening though, as Annabel fetched about five million magazines and proceeded to teach Becky "everything she needed to know". It took ages, and by the end of it Becky felt that there were so many things she had to remember when she saw David she wouldn't actually be able to spare any brain for thinking of what to say.

As it turned out, she saw Jack first, almost as soon as the triplets walked into the playground next morning. He was with a group of his mates, which was good, because when he saw all three triplets approaching he looked as though he might have dashed off if he'd been on his own.

"Hi Jack!" Becky was too full of how she was supposed to charm David to waste panicking time on Jack, so she just got straight to the point. "Listen, please can you just try and forget all that stuff Amy and Max were saying? They were just trying to stir up trouble, and I've got something really important to ask you." She took a deep breath, but Jack didn't seem to be about to yell at her or anything, so she went on. "I heard you might be getting rid of your rats, and I wondered if I could buy them off you, and the cage. I bet I could give you more than the exotic pet shop would."

Jack lost his hunted look and brightened up immediately. "Really? You've got the money? I bought them for twenty-five pounds with the cage."

"That's fine. Do you think you could bring them over on Saturday afternoon? We're having some friends round to watch videos, so I can give you the money and you could stay for tea if you like. Bring Robin, too, if he wants to come."

"Yeah, OK, I'll ask my mum. Excellent!" It was only as the triplets disappeared that Jack realized he should have asked for thirty...

Becky was desperate to find David and get it over with, but he didn't seem to be anywhere. They'd deliberately got to school early, to give her plenty of time – she wasn't sure she could face hanging around for ages. She had no nails left as it was. Suddenly Fran, who'd been filled in on the whole scheme as soon as she arrived, nudged her. "Look, he's over there!"

David was just walking in through the gate.

"Now Becky!" hissed Annabel. "Before he starts talking to someone or goes to play football or something. Go on!" And she pushed her sister hard in his direction, so Becky almost fell over. Somehow that push was very helpful – Becky turned round crossly to tell Annabel off, and caught the excited, incredibly Annabel-ish expression on her face. She suddenly realized that she didn't need to worry about all the stuff Bel had told her the night before. David didn't actually like her sister very much, or at least he never spoke to her. So why should she behave like Bel when she was talking to him? It was *Becky* he'd said was really sweet. She quickly banished all the stuff about looking up through her eyelashes and giggling in just the right way, and just went over to talk to her friend instead.

She walked over to him, grinning, and he saw her and smiled back – very nervously, but her grin was infectious.

"Guess what?"

"Er—"

"I've just bought Jack's rats off him, so he can't sell them off as snake food! Did you know he was going to do that? Can you believe it? I've been trying to work out a way to stop him all week. I'm going to get them off him on

Saturday afternoon – do you want to come round and see them? They're really gorgeous." Then she stopped to recover – she needed to breathe after rattling all that off.

"Um, yeah. That would be good," stammered David, his smile widening.

And then the bell went, and they actually walked into school together, talking about rats, and his pet gerbils, and Becky felt that maybe she could get used to this. . .

Saturday morning was less fun. Annabel seemed to have turned into a cross between a beauty therapist and a sergeant major, and she was not letting Becky out of her sight. She was all set to force Becky into wearing some of her clothes (which *she* was going to pick) until Katie rescued Becky by pointing out that she would be playing with the rats all afternoon, and did Bel really want rat all over her favourite top? Bel considered this with a horrified look on her face. Katie rolled her eyes sympathetically. She was quite enjoying not being the one that Annabel was bullying into dressing up.

They eventually settled on Becky's own denim skirt and gypsy-style top, and Becky let Annabel mess with her hair. She refused to wear as much make-up as her sister wanted – as she pointed out, it *was* fairly important that David recognized her. But Annabel still seemed quite pleased with her work as they stood at the front window, looking out for people to arrive. At least Becky had mascara on, for once.

"Look, that's Jack and his dad, with One and Two!"

Becky raced to the door. Jack had obviously scoured the cage that morning – it was practically sparkling – and his dad was carrying bags of food and bedding.

"Come on, I'll show you where to put them." She and Katie took the bags, and Mum took Jack's dad into the kitchen for a cup of tea.

Annabel followed upstairs, sighing. Somehow, she'd managed to forget just how *ratty* they were.

Soon all the others had arrived – Fran, Megan and Saima, Jack's friend Robin, and David, who had been really nervous until Becky met him on the stairs with a handful of wriggly cinnamon fur and thrust Two into his hands.

"What's she called?" he asked, trying to stop Two disappearing down his sleeve.

Becky stopped – she'd been taking him up to their room – and looked at him with eyes that were even huger and bluer than normal (Annabel was *good* at eye make-up). "I don't know! Oh, that's so silly! Jack just called them One and Two, but they have to have proper names now." Becky sat down on the stairs, and patted the step to get David to sit too. Then she laughed as Two decided this gave her an ideal opportunity to investigate David's hair. Becky grabbed for her at the same time as he did.

Annabel, hanging over the banisters on the

landing, nodded approvingly. She hadn't been convinced that Becky was listening on Wednesday evening, but there she was "accidentally" making physical contact, just like all the magazines said. Maybe even rats had *some* uses. . .

Becky and David grinned shyly at each other, and he moved closer to her on the step – just to make it easier to give Two back.

"So, what do you think you'll call her then?" he said quickly, to distract from being embarrassed about sitting so close. "She's a nice colour, maybe something to do with that?"

"Mmmm, maybe. Russet, or I could just call her Cinnamon, that's what this colour of rat's called. The other one's black and white, though, which isn't so good for names." Becky was chattering like that out of nerves, Annabel realized. And then she watched in delight as David clearly moved to hold her sister's hand!

Oh no! That *stupid* rat had staged an escape attempt, and Becky had moved her hand to catch it, so David had missed!

"Bel!" A furious hiss made her jump back as Katie grabbed her arm. "Stop spying, that's really awful!"

"I'm not! Well, OK, yes I am, but I just want to see if Becky's doing it properly."

"Well, you can't. Come on." And she dragged Annabel into their room, just as David put his arm around Becky.

Both David and Becky were very pink when they finally got to the triplets' room a couple of minutes later. And they hadn't got very far with names for the rats, either. Annabel smirked at Katie – they'd definitely held hands! And it was all down to her, she reflected with satisfaction. Well, maybe that was exaggerating a tiny bit, but Becky definitely couldn't have pulled it off on her own.

Katie managed a small grin back. She wasn't

totally sure what she felt about all this. Boyfriends were a whole new issue – especially *Becky* and a boyfriend. Would it mean her and Annabel and Becky spending less time with each other? A few weeks ago Becky had been the one complaining about that! Still, she thought, cheering up a bit, at least David probably wouldn't mind playing football with her every so often.

"So what are you going to call the rats?" Fran asked, watching Becky and David as she stroked One. She didn't have Annabel and Katie's inside information, but it was pretty clear that they were going to be an item. She was just glad David was nice – it would be awful if her best friend was going out with someone she didn't like.

Becky sighed. "No idea. Any suggestions?"

David grinned. "How about 'Amy' for one of them?" Then he ducked as everyone threw cushions at him. "Hey! Mind the rats, mind the rats!"

The triplets had done their best to get back at Amy and Max, but it hadn't been easy. It was all very well telling everyone what they'd done (as Katie said, it had been pretty terrifying to realize that they'd teamed up) but it just wasn't juicy gossip, like the rumour that Max and Amy had spread about Becky. Amy had seemed pretty surprised by the dirty looks that a few of the girls in the class had dared to give her, though, and some of the boys were ignoring Max after what David and Jack had told them. But the most annoying thing for Amy and Max was that Jack, David and Becky all seemed to be friends and the triplets were as popular as ever.

Becky smiled at Katie and Annabel. "Look, maybe you two should name them? After all, they are going to be sharing your room."

Katie looked thoughtful. "Pity they're both girls – makes it hard to name them after a footballer, or anything like that."

Becky sighed. "And I suppose you'd like to

call one after your favourite nail polish?" she said to Annabel.

Annabel raised her eyebrows. "Lilac Daze?" She looked down at One and Two rather sniffily. "I *don't* think so. Can I really name one of them?"

"Yeeees," said Becky doubtfully, wondering what she'd agreed to.

Annabel looked satisfied. "OK. That one," – she pointed at cinnamon Two, sitting on David's shoulder – "can be called Fang."

"Fang?" everyone echoed.

"Yes – it looks like a Fang. Horrible and toothy. Sorry, Becky, I'm *never* going to think they're cute."

Becky picked up One and held her in front of Katie. "OK. Your turn. Vermin? Ratbreath? What would you like?" she asked, sounding resigned.

Katie considered the black and white fur, and grinned. "Newcastle United. Cassie for short."

Becky rolled her eyes. Fang and Cassie? Oh well. At least it was a bit better than One and Two. She looked down at the rats – her rats – happily. She'd got just what she wanted – and more, she thought, as Fang whisked round and dived down David's top, and he rolled about the floor begging Becky to rescue him. . .

Look out for more

Triplets

HOLLY WEBB

Triplets

Becky's Terrible Term

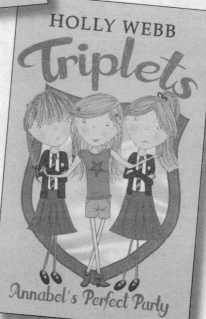

HOLLY WEBB

Triplets

Annabel's Perfect Party

HOLLY WEBB

Triplets

Katie's Big Match

HOLLY WEBB

Triplets

Annabel's Starring Role

HOLLY WEBB

Triplets

Katie's Secret Admirer

HOLLY WEBB

Triplets

Becky's Dress Disaster

Look out for